The Missing Link

Jessica Grundy

ISBN: 9781676506645

DEDICATION

I want to dedicate this book to Erika Klassen-Green. She was first, my friend. Then she became my cover artist, and now my editor. She also formatted this book for me. I owe this book to her because it would not have gotten published without her!

This one is for you, Erika. Thank you for everything!

CONTENTS

ACKNOWLEDGMENTS

As always. I am not the only one to help make the publishing of this book possible. There are so many people to give credit to, but I'm sticking to those who have been with me from the beginning. My Launch team (which is a group of five of my biggest supporters) who keep me on my deadlines and share the news of my books. My friends and family who have believed in and supported me since day one. To my cover artist, Erika, she carried this book for sure! And to anyone else who supports me, I love you and thank you.

PROLOGUE

Seven year old Clayton was sitting in his room watching cartoons when he heard his mom scream and something break. He walked slowly down the dark hallway to his parents room. As he got closer, he could hear what sounded like muffled screams coming from his mom. The door to their bedroom was half open, so Clayton was about to poke his head through. He was taken by surprise as the door flew open and he was face to face with his mom whose face was covered in blood.

"Get your sister and go to the car," yelled Ruby.

Scared, Clayton turned and ran to his sisters room. She was sitting up in her bed, obviously awakened by the commotion across the hall. She ran right to her brother, who picked her up, covered her with her favorite blankie, and took off out of the house; Ri'Lynn holding on tight. Once at the car, Clayton put his sister in her seat and buckled her up. He ran to the other side of the car and jumped in, anxiously waiting for their mom.

Finally, she stumbled out of the house and made it to the car, got in and sped off. Clayton knew his mom was hurt, but he didn't know where they were going or why they were going so fast. He looked over at his little sister who was squeezing her blankie so tightly her knuckles were white. As he reached over and grabbed her hand, another car had hit them, making them spin. Ri'Lynn let out a terrifying scream, gripping her brothers hand tighter as the car flipped and landed upside down.

"Clayton," came a whisper from his mom.

Clayton unbuckled and fell on the top of the car, glass cutting his skin. "Yes, Momma?"

"Please always…"

"Momma?"

"Look after your sister."

"I will. I promise, Momma," he said holding onto her hand until it went limp.

Shortly after he finished promising his mom, he heard sirens and saw the flashing lights. Within a matter of minutes, both him and his sister were pulled from the car and rushed over to the ambulance. Clayton sat there staring at the car knowing his mom was gone; knowing those were the last words his mother ever heard and the last words he'd ever speak to her.

Coming into the Light

Ri'Lynn stumbled into her room, hardly able to stand up straight; she was in so much pain. Shutting her door and locking it, she slid to the ground winching in pain. *Why is he doing this? Why does he hate me so much?* She asked herself these two questions every time her step dad hit her. Each time she was further from the answers than before.

She struggled to get up without her side hurting. Letting her body relax back on the floor, she had to think of a way to get up. Crawling to her bed, she took a deep breath which brought some pain itself, she stood to her feet, hand holding her left side. Her side was in so much pain; pain she'd never felt before. It hurt to breathe, to touch it, and bending was nearly impossible. She walked slowly over to her closet, stood in front of the mirror, and lifted her shirt, not recognizing her body. Eyes growing wide and filled with tears as she looked at her caramel colored side that was replaced with red and bluish, purple skin. *My step dad broke my ribs.*

It was only Tuesday and this was the third time he'd hit her. Ri'Lynn decided it was time to tell her step brother exactly how she was feeling about his dad. She didn't want to because she knew how close they were, but she was becoming more and more afraid of her step dad each day. Ri'Lynn paced the floor in the living room waiting for her brother to get home from football practice.

"Clayton, I don't think Adam likes me," blurted seventeen-year-old Ri'Lynn in a whisper, as soon as he walked in.

His pale face was red, hair matted to his face and he looked tired, but he smiled. “My dad does, too. Actually, he loves you. Why do you feel this way?”

Rilynn saw the instant sadness in her brother’s tired eyes. She wanted nothing more than to lift up her shirt showing him the bruises that made a home on her broken ribs caused by his father. She didn’t. She couldn't bring herself to tell him. She quickly changed the subject and rushed off to her room, shutting the door behind her. Throwing herself on the bed, she began crying wishing her mom was still alive because this wouldn’t be happening.

Clayton stood in the living room thinking about what his sister just said. He walked over to the couch, rubbing his hand through his hair. Why would Ri’lynn think his dad didn’t like her? He hadn't seen his dad be mean to her, although he never really paid much attention. He assumed his dad treated them both equally even though she wasn’t his biological daughter.

Adam cherished his son. He pushed Clayton to be the best in school, at sports, and in life. Clayton hated it at first, but quickly realized his dad just wanted what was best for him; it was done out of love. He figured his dad acted the same way with Ri’lynn, but was he wrong? Deciding to go talk to him, Clayton got up and walked to his dad’s office.

He plopped down in his favorite oversized chair, watching his dad work on his computer. Adam was a stocky guy in his mid-thirties who was a great, loving father. He didn’t just push Clayton to be the best football or baseball player. He supported him by showing up to every practice and never missing a game. As silly as he felt saying this out loud to anyone, his dad was like a best friend to him.

Clayton had tried numerous times to get his dad to start dating again and think about himself for a change. His dad made excuse after excuse as to why he couldn’t go on a date. Clayton felt sad his dad hadn’t dated anyone since his mom’s passing. All of his time was spent working and taking care of him and his sister. The rest of his time was spent making Clayton into the best athlete he could be.

He had always been able to talk to his dad about anything. Whenever something came up, good or bad, Clayton knew he could go to his dad for advice without any judgement. He hoped this conversation would be the same. One thing Clayton didn't tolerate is anyone messing with his sister. He made a promise to his mom, after all.

"What's up, kid" asked Adam, looking away from his computer.

"Nothing dad, just hanging out."

"We still up for the batting cages this weekend?"

"I was thinking. Why don't we all do something; the three of us?"

"I don't know, son. You really should practice."

"Dad, I practice all the time. It won't hurt me to miss a day or two," Clayton pressed.

"I don't think so," Adam admitted, agitated shifting in his seat,.

"Why not?"

"I just want to go to the damn batting cages with *my* son," yelled Adam as he slammed his fist on his desk. "I've got some work to finish up. Now get out."

Clayton sat there blinking repeatedly as his dad focused on his computer. He couldn't believe his dad got that upset over the suggestion for all three of them to do something. His dad couldn't be that upset about them not going to the batting cages, could he? No, because they canceled going all the time. It was something more, but what?

Getting up, he walked out of the room feeling perplexed. Was Ri'Lynn on to something about his dad not liking her? Why was his dad so upset? Was it *really* because he would be missing batting practice or was it something more? Unsure, Clayton went back to his room and turned on his PS4, determined to get to the bottom of this, but first he was gonna play a game with his friends.

Two weeks later, Ri'Lynn had just finished cleaning her room and was hungry. She stopped by her brother's room to see if he wanted anything to eat. Adam was working in his office and she knew he wasn't to be bothered. She quickly made them sandwiches and chips, taking Clayton his. Walking back to get her plate and drink, she jumped seeing Adam standing there in the hallway.

"What do you think you're doing?" questioned Adam.

"I made Clayton and I sandwiches. We were hungry."

"Where's mine?"

"You were in your office so I didn't want to disturb you."

"Well, I'm hungry. Make me a sandwich," Adam demanded.

"We are out of bread," Ri'Lynn admitted nervously.

"You're fucking kidding me, right?" yelled Adam.

Ri'Lynn just shook her head "no" without saying a word. That was a mistake. Adam became furious. He slapped her in the face, causing a red mark.

"Give me your sandwich, then," Adam demanded, hand out.

"But...but I haven't eaten all day. I'm starving."

Adam tried grabbing the plate from her, but Ri'Lynn didn't let go. This caused Adam to get even more angry and before she could let go, he pulled the plate out of her hand and dropped it; food and glass flying everywhere.

"Damnit, see what you did. Now nobody can eat. Clean it up."

"But you were the one… the one who dropped it," Ri'Lynn said, trying to stand up for herself.

Adam grabbed her arm and pulled her to him. His brown eyes black with rage, burned into her soul. When he spoke, although his voice was so low she could hardly hear him, his words trickled down her spine, sending a shiver through her body.

"Do not back talk me again, girl. When I tell you to do something, you stop what you're doing and do it."

Ri'Lynn didn't have time to respond before he grabbed the back of her neck and pushed her to the ground, pieces of the broken plate cutting into her knee. He was squeezing her neck hard but quickly let go when Clayton walked in the room.

"Dad, what happened here?" he questioned, looking at the mess.

"Oh I bumped into Ri'Lynn causing her to drop the plate. She was helping me clean it up."

Clayton looked at Ri'Lynn who shook her head yes.

"Here, why don't you use the broom instead," he said, handing it over.

"Thanks, I don't know why I didn't think of that," Ri'Lynn forced a laugh as she stood up.

"Ri, your leg is bleeding," Clayton said, pointing to her leg.

Ri'Lynn looked down and saw the blood running down her knee. She was so scared of what Adam was going to do that she didn't even realize her knee was getting cut by the glass. Thinking quickly, she propped up the broom and rushed off to the bathroom to clean her leg. She knew Adam wouldn't say anything in front of Clayton and she used that to her advantage to get away from him for a few minutes.

The cut on her leg wasn't big or even that bad. The blood dripping down her leg was the worst part. It didn't take her long to wipe away the blood and clean the cut. She put a bandaid on it and sat down on the edge of the bathtub, rubbing her hand over the back of her neck. *Why is Adam doing this?* She asked herself even though she knew she didn't know the answer. Taking a deep breath, she jumped up and willed herself out of the bathroom to clean up the mess.

Much to her surprise, the mess was cleaned up and the kitchen was empty. Adam had withdrawn back to his office and Clayton was probably back to playing his game. Ri'Lynn scurried off to her room, shutting and locking the door behind her. She hated the fact that she felt she needed to lock her bedroom door at night to feel safe, but it was the only way she could sleep.

Ri'Lynn woke in the middle of the night, stomach growling. Remembering she hadn't eaten all day, she crept out of her room and made her way into the kitchen. She quickly made herself a bowl of cereal and was heading back to her room when she noticed a figure standing in the doorway to her room. Her heart dropped into her stomach, then it started racing. She knew it was Adam coming to finish what he didn't get to earlier.

"What are you doing out of bed?" he asked.

"I...I am starving. I made myself a bowl of cereal," she said, taking a couple steps backward.

"I don't remember you asking."

"That's because I didn't. I didn't want to wake you."

"Looks like I'm awake. You still owe me from earlier."

"How do I owe you?"

"For one, I didn't get to eat my sandwich. For two, you got away without getting your punishment."

"I said I was sorry," Ri'Lynn said, her voice cracking.

"I don't care."

"I...I'll..I'll just put the cereal back and go to bed. I won't...I won't even eat it," said Ri'Lynn as she placed the bowl down on the counter.

The only way to get to her room was to walk past Adam, which she did quickly. But before she could get fully into her room, he grabbed her by the hair and threw her up against the wall. He grabbed both shoulders tight and pressed her body into the wall.

"I don't like you, I never have. You are a constant reminder of Ruby being unfaithful to me. She ruined our marriage. She's gone and I have to look at you everyday and I hate it. I hate it so much."

Ri'Lynn began to sweat. She could see the vein in his forehead pulsating up and down. He was pissed and she was about to feel it. She tried bracing for the punch, but no matter how much she prepared, it still hurt. He punched her in the side over and over like he always does. He was hitting her in the exact spot he hit her two days prior, the same spot her broken ribs lie. The pain almost tripled, causing her to yell out in agony as she slid down to the ground.

"Shut up. Shut up before you wake Clayton," Adam hissed.

"Please… please stop hit...ting...me," stuttered Ri'Lynn.

Adam balled his fist and raised his arm behind his head ready to strike her again…

"Dad, stop," hollered Clayton putting himself between them.

Adam stopped, his fist mid swing, "Boy, I almost hit you."

"Ri'Lynn, are you okay? Do I need to take you to the hospital?" Clayton asked, helping his sister up and looking her over.

"I'll be fine," she lied, waving him off. "I'm just gonna go to my room and lay down."

"Okay, go head to your room. I'll be there in just a second."

Clayton followed his dad and busted into his dad's bedroom, slamming the door open, fists balled. "What in the hell is your problem, Dad?"

"I don't have a problem, Clayton."

"The hell you don't. You must if you hurt your daughter like that."

"She is not my daughter. Now, watch your tone, boy."

"But that's your wife's daughter. She is my sister.'

"Son, your mother stopped being my wife the day she cheated on me with that black man. I wouldn't expect you to understand."

It finally clicked. "You don't have an actual problem with *Ri'Lynn*, you have a problem with her being biracial."

"White people belong with white people. Black people need to stop trying to infiltrate our race."

"Dad, you sound crazy; this isn't war. But I will tell you what will be war: if you ever put your hands on my sister again, it'll be a war between you and me."

Clayton walked out of his dad's office, leaving him mouth agape, speechless. Grabbing an ice pack from the kitchen and going into his sister's room, causing her to jump.

"Sorry Sis, I didn't mean to scare you. Here, put this on your side," he said, handing her the ice pack.and taking her hand. "I told him he better keep his hands off you. We can go to the hospital and file a report."

"No, we...we can't," Ri'Lynn stuttered, a shiver going over her body. "He will be so pissed off."

Clayton saw the fear in her eyes. "Okay Sis, we won't go. This time, but if he does it again, promise me you will agree to go?"

Knowing he would do it again, Ri'Lynn reluctantly promised her brother. She didn't want to give Adam any more reasons to put his hands on her even though she felt it wouldn't matter. He didn't need a reason to hit her. Since Adam's recent confession of his dislike for her, she knew any little thing could set him off. Going to the hospital, the police, or telling anyone else could be very dangerous for her.

"I promise, I will make sure he never puts his hands on you again."

Ri'Lynn smiled at her brother even though she knew he wouldn't be able to stop his dad from hitting her. She knew nobody could stop him. The only thing that could stop him is if she was no longer here. Or if he went to jail. Knowing neither would happen, Ri'Lynn laid down on her bed trying to escape her reality.

KNIGHT IN SHINING ARMOR

Clayton didn't know how to keep his promise to his sister aside from making sure she was never alone around his dad. He didn't know how long these beatings had been going on, but he assumed awhile since Ri'Lynn made the comment months ago about his dad not liking her. He had asked Ri'Lynn to wait until after his baseball practice before she went home even though he didn't like her having to sit there for a couple hours after school. She said she had no objections because she liked watching him and a couple of his teammates practice anyway.

When they were at home, Clayton made sure to not wear his headphones when he's playing his PS4 and keeps his door open all the time. He made sure he was always in the same room as his sister when his dad was out of his office. He even stopped hanging out at his friend, Tommy's as much, which was okay because his mom was real sick. Clayton was doing everything he could to protect his sister from his dad, but he was exhausted.

At times like this, he really wished his mother was around; he needed her so badly, and Ri'Lynn needed her more. Now, he felt fear: fear he wouldn't be able to protect his sister. Fear of breaking his promise to his mom. Fear of disappointing his dad. Fear of his dad. Is this how his mother felt when she told his dad what she had done?

Clayton knew his dad was a horrible husband, but he wasn't always. His mom stuck by his dad even through the abuse because of the kids; she didn't want to break up their family. And because she was too scared to leave. He knew the story of what happened between his parents. He knew all about what his mom did that broke his dad's heart, but he didn't agree with his dad for the way he treated her.

One night his mom was out at a bar and happened to meet a guy. They had a one night stand; she got pregnant. She was excited to have another baby she told Clayton when he got older, but she was scared what his dad would do once he found out. She couldn't keep it from him because the guy she slept with was black, her husband is white.

Once she mustered the courage to tell his dad, he stopped talking to her. He slept on the couch and wouldn't be in the same room as her. He made it very clear that the baby was not ever gonna be his. When Ri'Lynn was born and his dad saw her, he snapped. That's when the beatings started. One night Clayton remembered his dad beating his mom so bad she was hospitalized. He broke her ankle, fractured her left wrist, and sprained her spine. The doctors couldn't believe she was alive, and the cops were ready to put him away for life, but there was one problem. His mom wouldn't say it was him who did it. Even though everyone knew it was her husband, without her statement, he would go free.

Clayton didn't think his dad ever hit another woman after that time, until Ri'Lynn. Clayton was too young at the time to help his mom, but he wasn't too young to help Ri'Lynn. Now he was old enough to make sure his dad got exactly what he deserved. Before that could happen, he needed to find some sort of help. When his dad was out of the house, Clayton slipped into his dad's room, leaving Ri'Lynn safely in her room. Even though his dad acted as if he hated his mom, he never got rid of her things. Clayton didn't know if it was because deep down he still loved her or if he was just too lazy to do it.

Clayton was trying to locate Ri'lynn's biological dad, but it wasn't like he had much to go on. Hoping his mom had the name of the man or his phone number somewhere, Clayton looked through anything that he knew was his mom's. He went through box after box before he finally came across an address book. He assumed his mom had given Ri'Lynn her dad's last name because it was different than his. He looked through the address book until he found a Derek Reid. He tore out the page and put the boxes back, and then ran off to his sisters room.

"Hey Ri, how would you feel about meeting your biological dad?" blurted Clayton, excitedly.

"My *biological* dad? Are you trying to get rid of me?" she laughed.

"Ri'Lynn, you know I would never want to get rid of you.That is the *last* thing I want to do honestly," Clayton said, walking to and looking out of the window. His voice lowered as he admitted, " I just need help; I can't protect you by myself. And to be honest, if anything happened to you, I'd be devastated."

"What do you think meeting my biological dad would do?"

"I don't know, really. Maybe he can give you a place to stay if I can't be home. Or maybe he can give some advice as to what we should do."

"How would we even know how to get ahold of him?"

"I found a number in mom's address book," said Clayton, holding up a piece of paper.

"How do you know that he still has that number?"

"I don't, Ri. But honestly, I'm desperate. I'm exhausted and need help."

A LOST RELATIONSHIP

It had been a good three weeks since Clayton brought up to his sister about meeting her dad. She wasn't against it, but she was very nervous. Clayton promised, when she was ready, he would go with her. Until then, he tried to see if he could even find the man. Pulling the contact information from his wallet, he sat down on his bed, took a deep breath, dialed the number, and waited for what felt like an eternity.

"Hello?" a deep voice on the line snapped Clayton back to reality.

"Is this Mr. Derek Reid?"

"It is, who's asking?"

"My name is Clayton Bell, Sir. May I ask, do you know a Ruby Bell?"

The line went silent. Sweat started rolling down the side of Clatyon's face. Was this his number?

"Hello, Mr. Reid?"

"I'm here. Sorry, Clayton. You caught me off guard by asking about Ruby. I do know a Ruby Bell."

"If I may also ask, do you have a daughter with Ruby?" questioned Clayton, palms sweating.

"I do. Is Ri'Lynn okay?" asked Derek in a slight panic.

"Wait, you knew about Ri'Lynn?" Clayton questioned, breathing quickened and heart racing.

"I did. Is my daughter okay?"

"Yes, she is. Well sort of. I'm sorry, but I would rather talk with you in person about this."

"I don't know, man. I'm sure her parents wouldn't like that."

"I can assure you it won't be an issue. Please, Mr. Reid It's an urgent matter."

"Okay kid, you've convinced me. Where do you want to meet and when?"

"Tomorrow. Lunchtime. El Mezcal."

"Taking me on a date?" Derek laughed.

"Funny, but no. That's where I work on weekends. I'll be wearing a blue jacket. See you then."

"See ya, kid."

Clayton hung up and collapsed back onto his bed. He was more nervous during that phone call then he was when he had a couple big scouts watching his games. Collecting himself, he went to tell his sister of the conversation.

"Wait, he knew about me already?" Ri'Lynn questioned, confused.

"As soon as I mentioned mom's name he instantly asked if you were okay."

"Why haven't I ever met him? Maybe he didn't want me," Ri'Lynn hung her head.

"Ri, I don't think that's it. There's a lot going on that we don't know about. But don't worry, I will find out tomorrow."

"I want to go, but I don't want to be with you. I want to watch from a distance. Then you can call me over if he wants to meet me, okay?"

"Okay sis, but of course he wants to meet you. Who wouldn't?" he asked pinching her cheek.

Rolling her eyes, she pushed her brother out of her room. She sat there thinking about what it would be like to meet her dad as she did many times before. Would he be tall? Would he be handsome? Would she look like him? She spent the rest of the night wondering about what tomorrow would bring, pretty positive sleep wouldn't come easy. Unknowing to her, Clayton lay in his bed thinking the same exact thing, except he was also scared.

He was scared because what if the way Derek wanted to help Ri'Lynn was to have her move in with him and his family? What if Ri'Lynn wanted that? What if he lost his sister in an effort to save her? Unable to shake that feeling in his gut, he slid out of bed and turned on his PS4 hoping at least someone was online to play a game of Madden.

The next morning, much to his surprise, Clayton was fully rested despite only getting a couple hours of sleep. He knew it was due to him being just as nervous as his sister. Trying not to make this about him, he jumped out of bed and headed to take a shower. Passing his sister's room, he saw she was already dressed and ready.

"Damn girl, how long have you been up?" he said, laughing.

"I couldn't sleep so figured I'd get ready. You're up early, yourself."

"I couldn't sleep either."

"Clay, thank you so much. No matter how this goes, I really appreciate you doing this for me."

"For you? I'm doing this so I can take hot showers everyday," he joked as he walked out of his sisters room.

Right as they were about to walk out of the door, Adam yelled for Clayton which caused Ri'Lynn to jump.

"Yeah?" Clayton yelled back.

"Where do you think you're going?"

"Ri'Lynn and I are just going out to lunch," Clayton responded, pulling his sister out of the door, not giving his dad a chance to object.

Once they arrived at the restaurant, Ri'Lynn suggested she go in first and sit at a table towards the back, then he follows and sits at a table close enough she could see what was going on. With no objection from her brother, she climbed out of his Jeep and headed in to find her table. Shortly after, Clayton came in and found his table and waited; his leg nervously bounced up and down. His phone vibrated and hoped it wasn't Derek canceling. It wasn't. It was his sister texting him.

What if he doesn't show?

Ri, he will.

How long are you going to wait?

As long as I need to.

Omg. A man just walked in.

He's walking in your direction.

*Omg. Is that **him?***

Ri, shut up lol

Clayton didn't see what his sister had responded with because he put his phone in his pocket and stood to greet Derek, hand out ready to shake. Derek met his hand with a firm shake and they both took a seat.

"Care to tell me why you've called me here?" questioned Derek right away.

"No room for small talk, eh," laughed Clayton, nervously. "Okay so I'm just gonna lay it all out there and we will go from there."

When Derek didn't object, Clayton continued. "My dad, he beats Ri'Lynn. She doesn't feel safe at home, and I can't always protect her."

"What are you wanting me to do, kid? Beat up your dad? Where's your mom? Why isn't she stopping how her husband is acting?"

"My mom is… well my mom passed away."

"Wait, she passed away? When?" Derek asked shocked.

"Yes, she passed away when Ri'Lynn was five; I was seven."

"Wow. I am so sorry to hear that, kid. What happened, if you don't mind me asking?"

"We were in a car accident. I also vaguely remember my mom being beat up. I think she was driving to the hospital that night."

Derek ran his hands over his head, down to his neck. "I am really sorry. What can I help you with, Clayton?"

"Well Mr. Reid, I honestly have no idea. I have no clue how to handle this and Ri'Lynn won't let me go to the cops. He doesn't like her because she's mixed and not his daughter. Thought maybe if she got to know you… I just kind of need an adult to help us figure it out. I don't know. Maybe you could give me some advice if nothing else."

Derek looked at this defeated young man in front of him. His heart ached for him and for a daughter he never even met. Knowing he should probably call his wife first, his mouth opened before he could pick up his phone. "Is Ri'Lynn here? I'd like to meet her."

Clayton smiled, pulled out his phone, and called his sister over.

Derek gazed up and saw a beautiful light skinned young lady walking towards them. He loved the way her curls bounced with each step she took. He knew he was looking at Ri'Lynn because she had his hazel eyes and her mother's chunky cheeks. He couldn't believe how much she resembled her grandma, too. Before he could stand, she slid into the booth next to her brother, forcing him to scoot over which made Derek smile.

"Hello, Ri'Lynn. It's so nice to finally meet you," started Derek, breaking the awkward silence.

"Hi. Nice to meet you, too," Ri'Lynn looked away, palms sweating. "I know this was awkward, so thank you for coming."

"It did catch me off guard, but definitely not awkward by any means. I have dreamt of this day since I knew your mother was pregnant. I do want to say something before we continue," Derek paused and looked to Ri'Lynn, waiting for her to object. When she didn't, he continued, "I never wanted things to be this way. I wanted your mother to be with me. She was so terrified of her husband, she wouldn't leave him; even though we were madly in love. I wanted a life with her, with the three of us. I even told her she could bring her son. But she never came and once her husband threatened me, I stepped all the way back."

"Wait, my dad threatened you?" Clayton interjected.

"He did and I know I shouldn't have let that prevent me from being a part of my daughter's life. However, your mom told me that me stepping back was what was best. She said I needed to forget her and Ri'Lynn even existed. I was torn because I wanted nothing more than to be in my daughter's life, but I didn't pursue it any further."

Ri'Lynn blinks repeatedly, trying to process what she had just heard. She couldn't believe it! Her whole life she tried to figure out why her mom never let her know who her dad was, but not once did any of that cross her mind. She was never angry at her dad for being absent in her life, just confused. Didn't he care about her?

Ri'Lynn was indifference towards her mom for not leaving her information on her dad. She felt her mom would have told her everything had she gotten the chance, but she passed away before Ri'Lynn was old enough to understand. She didn't dare ask Adam anything because even if he did know anything, she didn't think he'd tell her because he didn't like her. That alone made her built up anger she didn't know she had.

All her anger was towards Adam. Angry because he altered her life, angry because he hits her, angry because she didn't do anything to deserve this. She was angry for what he did to their mother. But what made her the most angry was everything Clayton had been through. He saw how his dad treated their mom and now he was seeing his dad do the same thing to his sister.

Ri'Lynn wished he never had to witness any of this. He was forced to feel things and take responsibility for things he shouldn't have to. She hated that he was feeling helpless and that his good relationship with his dad was about to become tested because of helping her. But things were about to change for the both of them and she could feel it.

A NEW BEGINNING

After lunch, Derek went home to his wife, Angela, who was doing dishes. He stood there in the doorway to the kitchen leaning against the wall admiring her. Her brown curly hair hung down the middle of her back, thin waist, and that voluptuous booty. For being thirty six with her light skin tone, she aged well, keeping her body in shape after having two kids. Derek, who felt he wasn't as lucky with hiding his age, smiled thinking about how lucky he was to have her.

"Are you gonna speak, or just stand there?" she asked pulling him out of his thoughts.

"Sorry, I was just looking at how sexy my wife is standing there almost up to elbows in soapy bubbles, making our dishes shine," he joked, walking up behind her he kissed her neck.

"Yeah, yeah, so are you gonna tell me where you've been?" Angela questioned wiping her hands on a towel.

"Yeah, I will. Come have a seat."

"Oh hell, what did you go and get yourself into this time, Derek?"

"Hey, your husband is an angel," he laughed as he batted his eyes. "Anyway, I got a strange phone call yesterday. One I never thought I'd get. Do you remember the woman I told you about who I got pregnant, but she was married and didn't want anything to do with me?"

"Yeah, I remember." Angela's body stiffened.

"Her son reached out to me on behalf of my daughter. I went and met with them today. Now, don't get all upset because I didn't talk to you about it first. I just wanted to check and see what was up before I involved you."

"Okay, so how did it go?" she calmly asked.

"So Clayton, Ruby's son and my daughter's half brother, met me first. He told me that his dad, he has been beating her."

"Beating her? Oh my goodness. What is her mother doing about that?"

"She actually passed away when they were younger. If I remember correctly, Ri'Lynn was five and Clayton seven."

"Oh my gosh! I couldn't imagine leaving my babies that young in life; or ever actually. Was she sick?"

"No, actually they got into a car accident and she didn't make it."

"Both the kids were in the car, too?" asked Angela, hand covering her mouth.

"Yes, they were. Clayton said he vaguely remembered his mom being beat up. Her husband beat her bad enough that she tried to take the kids and drive to the hospital and that's when they were in a car accident and she didn't make it."

Neither one of them said anything, both lost in their own thoughts. Derek had always hoped his daughter had an easy and happy life. Never did he think her life had had so much trauma. He wanted nothing more than to pluck her out of that life and give her a better one.

"Ruby's husband used to beat her because she got pregnant by you?" His wife asked him a question, which pulled him out of his thoughts.

"That's what I think. I know she was terrified of him when I met her, but she never said he was physically abusive."

"So it seems like after she had Ri'Lynn he became abusive."

"Yeah, that's what it seems like. I don't know when the beating started for Ri'Lynn, but I imagine it's because she isn't his. Unless he just doesn't like women."

"That is horrible. I wouldn't know what I'd do if anyone ever touched my babies," Angela admitted, breathing quicking.

"Angela, you know I would never lay a hand on you or our kids, right?"

"Yes, I know you wouldn't, baby," Angela leaned in and kissed him passionately. "What did they want you to do?"

"To be honest, they don't really know. Clayton was just trying to protect his sister and didn't know what else to do. I mentioned calling the cops, but Ri'Lynn was too scared of what her step dad would do if they did that. I don't know what to do either, but I want to start getting to know her and help them. I also want to make sure you and the boys are gonna be okay with all of this."

"Baby, we will do whatever we need to do not only to help her, but so you can get to know your daughter. And I'm sure the boys would love to have a big sister."

"Angela, this is why you are my queen and I love you so much," said Derek, a tear running down his cheek.

"I love you too, my king."

****

Since their lunch, Ri'Lynn had been in constant contact with her dad. She was worried it would feel awkward, but it actually felt normal. She couldn't believe how talking to him made her so much more happy. She noticed her brother was acting a little different since that day, so she decided to talk to him and see what was up. She jumped up from her bed and ran to her brothers room. He was lying on his bed, headphones on, eyes shut. She jumped over him and laid next to him, startling him.

"What's up, brother?"

"My heart rate," Clayton laughed, gripping his chest. "What's up, girl?"

"So you've been acting strange ever since we met my dad. What's up with that?" Ri'Lynn blurted out.

"Um, well. I don't know," mumbled Clayton, breaking eye contact.

Ri'Lynn sat up on the bed and looked at him. "Clay, what's going on. You can talk to me."

"I know I can, but it's no big deal."

"Clay, come on."

"Ri'Lynn, it's really no big deal. I am fine, it's just a little funk."

"I don't believe you one bit," she said, crossing her arms.

"I'm scared I'm gonna lose you," he finally admitted.

"Lose me? Why or how would you lose me?" Ri'Lynn asked, sitting up.

"I don't know. What if you get close enough to your dad and you want to leave?

Ri'Lynn's heart broke. "Clay, even if I did leave, I would never, ever leave you. We are way too close for me to just leave and cut you out of my life."

"That means a lot to me, sis. I just don't want anything to happen to you for me to lose you. Whether it be because you move with your dad, or because my dad is an asshole and hurts you."

"Clay, I want you to know I don't blame you for how your dad is treating me."

"I just feel horrible about it."

"Don't. You didn't do anything wrong at all. All you want is what's best for me. Besides, you brought me and my dad together and for that I am forever grateful." Ri'Lynn grabbed his hand and squeezed. "Clay, we can get through anything together."

****

"Honey, how would you feel about meeting my daughter?" Derek asked as he and his wife cuddled in bed.

"I would love to, baby."

"Bet. I'll talk with the boys in the morning."

Derek woke up the next morning with his heart happy; the last seventeen years, he had a hole in his heart. He tried not to think about missing the birth of his daughter, about not holding her, about all the doctor appointments he missed. Those feelings alone were enough to bring him to tears. He, at one point, did love Ruby. He wasn't madly in love with her at the time, but knew it would be easy to fall head over heels for that woman. He didn't like that he messed with a married woman. He hated that she stayed with her husband

and allowed him to treat her the way he did. But she broke his heart, twice.

He didn't know how to explain to his boy's, who were both under ten, that they had a big sister. Nor did he know how they would take it. He wanted them to know her and he wanted his wife to get to know her, too. Most of all, he wanted to get to know her. Derek didn't know where things would go. He wanted to get his baby girl out of that house as soon as possible but his priority would need to be his sons.

Derek called Brian and Daniel into the living room and gently told his six and eight year old about their twenty year old sister, Angela right there next to him. He left out the details of how he met Ruby, but he made sure they knew it was well before their mother. He also made sure they knew Ruby and her husband had issues and didn't want him to be a part of Ri'Lynn's life and that's why they didn't know about her. He let it all sink in a little before he asked them how they felt.

"A big sister? I can't wait to meet her," Brian said excitedly.

"Girls are gross. I don't want anything to change. She won't be living here with us, will she?" questioned Daniel.

"For right now, she will be staying where she lives. But, her stepdad is a mean man and has been hurting her. If we get to know her, she could possibly come stay with us."

Brian jumped up and down with excitement. Daniel wasn't as excited. "I don't want her to stay with us. I don't want her breaking up our family!"

"Baby, our family won't be breaking up; it will be growing," reassured Angela.

"But I don't want it to grow!" spat Daniel. "I like things the way they are right now."

"You don't have a choice, son," Angela said, placing her hand on his shoulder. "She is your sister and if she needs our help, we will help her. Your dad wants to get to know his daughter, he's missed her very much. He would like it if we could all get to know her as well."

"Fine, but it doesn't mean I'm gonna like her."

He got up and stomped off to his room, slamming the door behind him. Angela got up to go after him, but Derek told her to let him cool off. Brian skipped off to his room, happy as can be. At least one of his boys was happy and that was more than Derek expected.

"How are you feeling about this and don't lie to me?" Derek asked his wife after the boys were gone.

"I'd never lie to you, baby," winked Angela. "Derek, if this is what you want, I will stand behind you. I'm sure the boys would love having a big sister to torment. It's just gonna take Daniel a little longer to get used to the idea. I know I'd love to have a daughter to do girly things with."

"I love hearing that, Angela."

"Baby?"

"Yes, my queen?"

"Don't you dare blame yourself for any of this. You're a good man and a great father. You would have been a great father to her if you'd gotten the chance. I know you've been hurting for awhile, but do not let this situation add to that pain. Let it heal your broken heart and make up for lost time and get your daughter away from that man."

****

Ri'Lynn was sitting in her room doing homework when she heard the front door open and shut. Thinking it was her brother, she kept on with her homework. A few minutes later, she heard stomping footsteps heading straight for her room. Turning around she saw a very pissed off Adam storm into her room. Before she could say anything, he snatched her by the ponytail pulling her into the kitchen.

"What the hell is wrong with this picture, Ri'Lynn?" he demanded pulling tighter on her hair as she struggled to get away.

"The dishes aren't done, but I was going to do them after I finished my homework."

"Are you saying that doing your homework is more important than doing what I told you to do?"

"It's kind of a big assignment, and I thought maybe it was more important for me to study than do the dishes," Ri'Lynn said softly.

Adam was not happy with her answer and slapped her across the face with his free hand. Letting go of her ponytail to hit her in the ribs, she took a hit and ran. She was almost at the door when Adam grabbed the back of her shirt and threw her against the wall. He busted her lip and wrapped his hands around her neck.

"When I tell you to do something, you do it then; not when you want to."

Before anything else could happen, the front door opened and in stepped Clayton and his best friend, Tommy.

"Dad, what the hell?" yelled Clayton as he ran to his sister, and pulled his dad off of her.

Adam was still so fired up he was trying to grab her, but Clayton held him back. "Tommy, get my sister out of here. Take her to your house and I'll be down there soon."

Tommy did as his best friend ordered and dashed to Ri'Lynn's side. He helped steady her and rushed her out of the house. She was holding her ribs and moving slowly so Tommy picked her up and jogged the four houses down to his house; her head on his chest. Once at his house and on the porch, he gently put her down. As he unlocked the front door he took her hand and led her inside to the bathroom right past his mom. Seeing a bloody Ri'Lynn with her son, caused her to jump up and follow them.

"Tommy, what happened to her?"

"It's okay, Mom don't worry yourself. Let me get her cleaned up first and I'll tell you," Tommy said shutting the door to the bathroom.

"I'm sorry. I hope I didn't get you in trouble." Ri'lynn muttered through the waves of pain.

"Nah, it's okay. My mom is cool. Do you mind if I take pictures?"

"Pictures? Of what?" Ri'Lynn backed away from Tommy.

"Of your face and the handprint around your neck. You know, for proof in case you ever wanna go to the cops."

Ri'Lynn didn't answer right away. She sat there sitting on the toilet looking at the ground, not sure what to say. She'd been around Tommy as long as she could remember and never saw this side of him. For a big, tough football player, he was very compassionate. He made Ri'Lynn feel safe.

Lifting her head Tommy said, "I'm just gonna take a couple pictures because I know that's what Clayton would want." After snapping the pictures he goes, "Now let me clean you up."

Tommy took a cool washcloth and began wiping the blood off her face and the little that had dripped down on her chest. He was being as gentle as he could not wanting to cause her any more pain than she was already in.

"Did Clayton tell you about his dad?" she asked while he finished up.

"No, he never told me. I knew something wasn't right with him though. He never wanted to come over anymore and was always rushing to get home. I thought maybe I pissed him off. He did tell me about you meeting your real dad and I know how close y'all are so I thought that was it. I had no idea. I'm sorry, Ri'Lynn."

"Thank you so much for cleaning me all up. And for carrying me down here. You're pretty gentle for a football muscle head," Ri'Lynn smiled a little smile.

Tommy blushed, ignoring her comment. "Come on, you can wait in my room while I talk to my mom."

Tommy got her set on his bed with the TV remote in her hand. He went back to the living room and sat next to his mom who was waiting patiently to find out what happened. He told her he would only tell her if she promised not to get too worked up about it. He knew her health was bad enough without the extra stress. She agreed and he told her what happened.

Back at the house, Clayton was letting his dad have it.

"What is your problem, Dad? Seriously."

"She didn't do what I told her to do."

"Which was what?"

"The dishes."

"Come on, Dad. Really, the dishes? You acted like she robbed a damn bank. She was probably doing homework. You know if it was me, you would have wanted me to do my homework before anything else, right?"

"Well that's different," Adam tried to reason with his son.

"How? Tell me how that's different."

"Because you are my son."

"Dad, I am so sick of this shit. I can't believe you. I don't know who you are anymore."

"I am still the same dad I've always been," Adam pleaded with his son.

"No, you aren't and I don't like who you've become."

Clayton stormed out of his house and slammed the door. He ran to Tommy's house, knocking once before he went in. Ri'Lynn, Tommy and his mom were all in the living room. Ri'Lynn jumped up and limped into his arms, crying softly. He held her tightly and swayed back and forth apologizing over and over. He wanted to promise this wouldn't happen, but he didn't want to break that promise, again. He however, was getting more and more scared for the safety of his sister. Something had to be done; his dad needed to be locked up and he was gonna make it happen with or without Ri'Lynn's help.

Tommy's mom offered for them to stay the night and Clayton gladly accepted. The boys went back and grabbed a few things while Ri'Lynn helped Tommy's mom prepare dinner. She loved being around Tommy's mom; she was the sweetest lady ever.

"I just hate that he did that to you, Ri'Lynn."

"I know, Mrs. Judy but I'm okay. The boys got there in time and Tommy fixed me up pretty good."

"I'm glad they look after you. But I saw you limping and wincing in pain. What is that about?"

"I um… I'm quite positive my stepdad broke my ribs."

"He did? Oh sweetheart, you need to go to the doctor," pressed Judy.

"I'll be fine. The doctors couldn't do anything anyway." Changing the subject Ri'Lynn said, "Why don't you go sit down in the living room and put your feet up. I'll finish dinner."

"Ri'Lynn that is kind of you. I'll just sit here. I don't get to cook much these days. I used to love being in the kitchen. This chronic kidney disease gets the best of me sometimes."

They continued chatting while Ri'Lynn finished dinner. The boys came back and Tommy tried to convince his mom to move to the living room, but she refused because she wanted to stay with them in the kitchen. They all enjoyed a nice dinner at the table, laughing and enjoying the company. After dinner, Tommy took his mom to bed while Ri'Lynn and Clayton cleaned the kitchen. Once they finished, Clayton headed off to Tommy's room to study for a big test he had tomorrow.

Ri'Lynn was getting herself set up in the spare bedroom when she heard a slight knock on the door. It was Tommy.

"Hey Tommy."

"Hey Ri, I just wanted to thank you for helping my mom cook and chatting with her. She said it really made her feel good."

"Of course. You know I love your mom."

"Do you need me to get you anything?"

"I don't think so."

"If you need anything, come holler at me," he kissed her on the top of the head and walked out, closing the door behind him.

Ri'Lynn stood there smiling for a minute. She was really thankful her brother had such a great best friend and he had such a sweet mother. She changed into a t-shirt and a pair of shorts and dialed her own best friend's number. Since Lilly's parents divorced, she moved away with her mom so they didn't get to see each other anymore, but they talked almost everyday.

"Hey Ri, what's up?"

"Currently laying in Tommy's guest room."

"Wait, you're what!? Do tell me more and don't leave out any details."

Ri'Lynn laughed, loving how her best friend made her feel. She told her everything, even all the beatings she'd gotten before and hadn't told her about. Ri'Lynn also told her about how Clayton found her dad and she got to meet him and talks with him everyday.

"I cannot believe all of that, Ri."

"Yeah, a lot has happened since you left."

"I'll say. I wish I could come down there and punch Adam in his nuts. That's what you need to do next time he puts his hands on you; kick that man right in the nuts."

"Lilly, I wish I had your balls. When he hits me, I just freeze."

"What does your dad say about this?"

"Well, he doesn't like it, but he has a family of his own with two little boys, so it's not like I can just move in with him."

"Why not?"

"I mean, I guess I could. Adam hadn't hit me in awhile until today. I was working on getting to know my dad. He could be worse Lil, I don't know the man."

"Good point. I just worry about you."

"I know, but don't. I'll be okay. Besides, both Clayton and Tommy are looking out for me."

"They are your knights in shining armor."

They both laughed. Ri'Lynn asked questions about Lilly's new school and new friends. She wanted to know everything about her best friends new life. While listening to her friend talk, she wished herself and Clayton could pick up and start a new life themselves. Maybe having her dad come into their lives would be good for both of them and offer them just that.

CHANGE OF PACE

Since her last beating two months ago, Adam hasn't touched Ri'Lynn. She had been getting closer and closer to her dad and was finally going to meet her brothers and his wife.

"You know, they won't be as cool as me," Clayton said leaning against the window of his Jeep he was letting her borrow.

"You're right. They will be cooler," Ri'Lynn joked back rolling up the window.

Clayton stood there laughing as she drove away; a piece of her heart broke when she saw the smile leave his face. She wanted him to go with her, but she knew she needed to do this one alone. No matter how cool her younger brothers were, they couldn't replace Clayton and she was gonna make sure he knew that. Ri'Lynn pulled into the driveway of the address her dad gave her. She was astonished as she looked at the house in front of her. It was two stories high, with a two car garage. There was a beautiful garden full of flowers she'd never even seen before. The house looked so welcoming; so homey.

She turned off her car and walked up and rang the doorbell. Within a few minutes, she could hear rustling around inside and someone walking towards the door. The door opened, a beautiful macchiato toned skin woman with the prettiest smile stood in front of her.

"You must be Ri'Lynn," she said before Ri'Lynn could even muster the courage to speak. "Come on in, I'm Angela by the way. Did you find the house okay?"

"Yes ma'am, I did."

Ri'Lynn followed Angela through the small picture covered hallway, stealing glances at their lives and into the living room where her dad and two brothers were sitting. Her dad walked over and gave her a hug, while her two brothers sat nervously on the couch. Angela sat down next to her sons and Derek on the other side, Ri'Lynn sat in the chair across from the couch.

"Ri'Lynn, I'm so glad you could come. Dinner will be ready shortly," Angela said as a timer went off and she got up and walked into the kitchen.

"I'm also glad you could come too, Ri'Lynn. I've been telling your brothers a lot about you. They are a little shy, but they are excited to meet their big sister. This is Brian, he's six. This is Daniel, and he's eight."

Ri'Lynn smiled, feeling all warm inside. "I'm so excited to meet you two. I have a big brother, too."

"You do?" Exclaimed Brian.

"I do! He's pretty cool. He plays football and baseball."

"Did you hear that, Daniel? You like football!"

"Yeah I heard, so what?" spat Daniel.

"Daniel, be nice to your brother. Is there anything you want to ask your sister?" interjects Derek.

"She's. Not. My. Sister!" Daniel yelled haltingly then ran out of the room, slamming a door down the hall.

"I'm so sorry about that, I'll go talk to him," Derek said.

"If you don't mind, can I go talk to him?" asked Ri'Lynn.

"Of course," smiled Derek, telling her which room was his.

Ri'Lynn did a little knock then entered Daniel's room. He was not too happy to see her, making a scowl when he saw her.

"Hey Daniel, can we talk?"

"I guess," he mumbled as he crossed his arms looking away.

"I'm not mad at you for not wanting to call me your sister. You can just call me Ri'Lynn, if you want."

"Really?"

"Of course. This isn't easy for my brother either, so I know it's not gonna be easy for you guys. We can just take it little by little and get to know each other, okay?"

Daniel uncrossed his arms and looked at her. "I'd be okay with that, I guess. Why isn't this easy for your big brother?"

"Are you and Brian close?"

"I mean kinda. He can be annoying sometimes."

Ri'Lynn laughed. "All younger siblings can get annoying. I even annoy my brother sometimes, too. But him and I are really close; we are best friends. He's scared that you two will be so cool, I'll wanna spend all my time with you guys and not him. I just wanted you to know that we can be friends first, before brother and sister if you'd like. I'm gonna go back out in the living room and you can come out when your ready."

Derek and Angela, who had been listening in on their conversation, rushed back to the couch and sat down, making Brian laugh.

"What's so funny?" Ri'Lynn asked as she sat back down.

"Mom and dad listened to what you said to Daniel," blabbed Brian.

"Hey! You snitch," teased Derek.

They all laughed and talked for another twenty minutes until dinner was ready. Even Daniel came back and joined them. They had a wonderful dinner with lots of laughs. After dinner was finished, Ri'Lynn helped do dishes and then headed home. She couldn't wait to tell Clayton all about her evening.

Once home, she rushed into her brothers room only to find he wasn't there. Grabbing her phone to text him, she walked right into Adam who was coming out of the kitchen, making him drop his plate.

"Oh my gosh. I am so sorry, Adam. I didn't see you," Ri'Lynn said as she bent down to pick up the food.

"You were too busy on that damn phone. Where the hell have you been, anyway?"

"I ... uh was at a friend's for dinner."

"You didn't ask me if you could go to a friend's."

"I'm sorry, I'll remember to ask next time."

"The hell you will. There won't be a next time."

Ri'Lynn didn't object. She looked to the front door, but couldn't get to it without him getting to her first. Her only option was going to be the back door. She just had to get through the kitchen first. Without thinking anymore, she took off running into the kitchen, but Adam knew what she was going to do because he tripped her, causing her to fall face first in the middle of the kitchen.

Adam snatched her up on her feet by her shirt collar and smacked her across the face. She pushed him back against the counter, slightly catching him off guard. She tried to run, but he grabbed her, knocking her face into the kitchen counter. He pushed his body into hers and told her not to move.

Adam had his hand on the back of her neck, squishing her face into the counter; drawer knob stabbing her in the stomach. Ri'Lynn tried to adjust her body under his, which was a bad idea. He punched her in the side, screaming in her ear to stop moving. She heard him unbuckle his pants and they fell to the ground.

Ri'Lynn began to panic when she pieced together what he was about to do. She tried her hardest to fight him off, but he was way too strong. She cried and begged him to stop, but he kept forcing himself inside of her as if he didn't hear her. She tried to kick him, but couldn't reach. She landed a good elbow to the side before he held her arms above her head.

Ri'Lynn knew it was pointless to keep fighting and it was only going to hurt her even more. She tried to think of something, anything else; but she couldn't escape what was happening. She looked around the kitchen trying to focus on something different when she saw a reflection of them in the hallway mirror; she closed her eyes praying it would be over soon. After what felt like an eternity, he finished, releasing on her butt. She pulled up her pants and ran out of the house; she had to get away from that evil man.

She ran as fast as she could to Tommy's house praying that's where her brother was. She began banging on the door as hard as she could; scared Adam was following her.

"I'm coming, geeze," Tommy yelled from the other side.

"What the hell..." he started to ask but quickly pulled Ri'Lynn inside and shut the door. "Ri'Lynn, what happened?"

"Is my brother here, please tell me my brother is here?"

"Yeah, he's here. Come on, he's in my room."

Tommy helped her walk to his room. She was thankful for Tommy being so helpful.

"Bro who the hell was beating on your door like the Police?" Joked Clayton.

"Clay," was all Tommy said before Clayton turned around, jumped up and ran to his sister who leapt into his arms.

"Ri'Lynn, are you okay? Please tell me you didn't go home? I messaged you telling you to come here instead."

"I didn't see the message in time."

Looking her over, he asked, "Where did he hit you this time? Where does it hurt?"

Ri'Lynn didn't say anything she just shook her head. "Clay, we need to call the cops," she managed to mumble.

"Call the cops? I thought you didn't want to do that?" asked Clayton confused.

Ri'Lynn stepped back from her brother and wiped her face. She grabbed his hands and said, "Clayton, your dad…"

She couldn't finish what she was going to say. She could feel her stomach doing all kinds of somersaults. Running off to the bathroom, she barely made it to the toilet before she got sick. Throwing up for a good five minutes straight, Ri'Lynn felt weaker than before and she didn't think that was possible. She stood up on shaky knees and splashed water on her face before she sat down on the floor, leaning against the bathtub. Within minutes of her sitting down, both her brother and Tommy came to check on her.

"Ri, are you okay? Tell me what is going on."

Ri'Lynn looked at her brother standing there in front of her. She didn't want to tell him. She didn't want to see what this was going to do to him. But she had to tell him. She needed him to help her get through this.

"Clay. Your dad...he... just raped me," Ri'Lynn said through tears.

Tommy's mouth dropped. Clayton's heart skipped a beat and he fell to his knees, head in his hands, crying. Ri'Lynn scooted herself next to him, wrapping her arms around him, crying too. Tommy left the room, hands shaking and called 911.

When the cops arrived, Clayton didn't leave his sister's side. He held her tight as they brought his dad out in handcuffs and placed him in the back of the squad car. He rode with her to the hospital, Tommy following in his car. Once they got to the hospital, the boys had to wait outside while they did a rape kit on Ri'Lynn.

"Bro, you okay?" Tommy asked nervously.

"Man, I just can't believe it. I cannot believe my dad would be this cruel, man. She's been through so much already. I can't believe he would do this to her."

"Do you think you should call her Dad?"

"Shit bro, you are right. He totally slipped my mind," Clayton ran his hands through his hair. "Stay right here while I go call him. Do not leave this spot for any reason and call me if anything is going on."

"Okay bro, I'll be right here."

Clayton hugged his best friend and walked out of the hospital. He pulled his phone out of his pocket and called Derek.

"Hey Derek, this is Clayton. Do you have a minute?"

"Sure, give me a second to get to my office." After a few minutes he got back on the phone. "Go ahead Clayton, what's up?"

"Are you sitting down?"

"I am."

"I think, if you have the time, you should come to the hospital. Or send your wife."

"Clayton, what happened?!"

"My dad...he...uh..." Clayton struggled getting the word out of his mouth. He still couldn't believe this was real. "He raped her."

The line was silent. Clayton's mind raced. The tears started to flow as he replayed the words his sister told him. He was so caught up in his own head, he didn't even hear Derek talking to him.

"Clayton, son. Are you okay?"

"Huh? Sorry, I'm fine."

"I know that's a lie obviously you're not fine and that's okay. I can tell you really love your sister. I have a meeting in about ten minutes that I can't miss. I will send my wife up there now, then I will be there as soon as my meeting is over."

"Thank you, Derek."

Derek hung up and immediately dialed his wife, telling her what happened. She told him she'd head up right away. He thanked her and walked into his meeting with a heavy heart, his mind in another place. Meanwhile, Angela rushed into the hospital, walking right up to Clayton and Tommy.

"You must be Derek's wife," Clayton said, extending his hand.

"Angela and you must be Clayton."

He nodded. "This is my best friend, Tommy."

They chatted for a few minutes before Angela stopped a nurse to ask about going into the room with Ri'Lynn. The nurse looked to Clayton to confirm then took Angela into the room with Ri'Lynn.

Ri'Lynn was sitting on the bed, curled into a ball rocking back and forth, crying softly. When the nurse touched her she jumped off of the bed and ran into the corner of the room. Once she locked eyes with Angela, she cried out and ran into her arms.

"Has the rape kit already been done?" Angela asked the nurse.

"Yes, just waiting on the detective to come get her statement, then she can leave."

Angela sat down on the hospital bed with Ri'Lynn and held her hand as the detective came in and she gave her statement. After the detective got the information, she asked Angela to step outside with her.

"Ri'Lynn said Adam was her stepdad, are you her mother?" asked Detective Hernandez.

"No, ma'am I am not. I am Ri'Lynn's biological father's wife."

"Do you know if Clayton's mother is around?"

"She passed away when they were younger."

"Do you know if he has any other family around?" questioned the Detective.

"Why are you asking about my family?" interrupted Clayton who had been listening.

Turning to him, Detective Hernadez answered. “You are a minor and if there is no other family members available for you to stay with, you will need to be placed in a home for the time being.”

Clayton’s mouth dropped. Angela squeezed his shoulder. “With all due respect, ma'am, what Clayton needs is to be with his family. We might not be his biological family, but we are family nonetheless. His dad just got arrested and his sister assaulted. He’s been through enough no need to tear them apart. Ri’Lynn and Clayton have had a long day and need to go home and rest. You can send child services to our house and we will fill out whatever paperwork is necessary for the kids to stay with us. Now if you’d excuse us.”

Clayton was impressed with how Angela handled that. He hadn’t even thought about what would happen to him now that his father was in jail, but he was glad Angela was there to take care of that for him. With Angela leading the way, the three of them went to their house and packed a couple bags. Clayton packed his and helped his sister with hers. They loaded up and headed to Angela's where Derek was waiting.

Clayton helped his sister get out of the car and into the house while Angela grabbed their bags. Ri’Lynn hadn’t said a word since she stopped talking to the detective at the hospital but she squeezed onto Clayton’s hand tightly as they walked inside the house.

“Ri’Lynn…” Derek started but couldn’t finish because he got choked up.

Angela noticed and stepped in. “Clayton, why don’t you take Ri’Lynn to the back bedroom. You can have the one across the hall. I will call you guys when dinner is ready.”

“Thank you,” said Derek after they were gone.

“Of course. But baby, social services are gonna pay us a visit soon.”

“Social services? Why?” a concerned Derek asked.

“Because Adam went to jail and Ruby passed away, they needed to place Clayton with family. Since there isn’t any, they want to put him in a foster home.”

“Foster home? No way. He can just stay here with us.”

"That's what I told the detective. Told her to send the case worker to the house and we will fill out whatever paperwork needed to make sure both of the kids stayed with us."

Derek plopped down on the couch, resting his head on the back of it and just stared at the ceiling. "Thank you so much for going today and for speaking up on Clayton's behalf. I know that'll mean so much to Ri'Lynn. I wanted nothing more than to be there myself. I feel like I let her down again."

"We are family and family sticks together, no matter what." Angela pulled his body upright and took his face in her hands. "Baby, you didn't let her down at all. She's gonna need you now more than she has her whole life. Why don't you go talk to her?"

Derek kissed his wife on the forehead and headed off to the back bedrooms. He checked on Clayton first making sure he didn't need anything. When he didn't, Derek walked across the all to Ri'Lynn's room, knocking twice before entering. Walking in the room was dark except for a lamp that was on the nightstand next to the bed. Ri'Lynn lay on the bed curled up in a ball, facing the wall.

Derek stood there looking at his daughter, heart breaking. She looked so small and childlike. He wanted to grab her and wrap his arms around her and tell her he wouldn't ever let anyone hurt her again. Instead, he sat down on the bed and placed his hand on her leg to get her attention. She flinched and scooted to the top of the bed in the corner. Derek saw so much fear in her eyes and her body tremble. He stood up and backed away slowly, tears running down his face.

"I'm... I'm sorry, Ri'Lynn. I didn't mean to," Derek said as he rushed out of the room.

"Dad, wait," Ri'Lynn called even though she knew he wouldn't hear her.

****

Once Tommy had gotten home from being at the hospital with his friends, it all finally hit him and he shed a tear or two. He couldn't believe Adam. He never seemed like the abusive type; Clayton hardly got any whoopings growing up. Tommy loved spending time with Clayton and his dad. They did all kinds of things together; batting cages, hunting, fishing. All kinds of things he couldn’t do with a dad because his own dad had passed away.

Unable to wrap his head around what would make Adam go that far and rape his own stepdaughter, Tommy’s head hurt. He didn't tell his mom what was going on because he knew that would really upset her. She couldn’t handle it and she needed to remain calm. Her sickness was taking a turn for the worst. With everything going on, Tommy didn't know how much longer he'd be able to hold it together before he snapped.

UNEXPECTED VACATION

Derek was up early in his office working. With everything that happened the day before, he couldn't sleep. Him and Angela agreed to let Brian and Daniel stay home from school today, along with Clayton. Nobody knew when Ri'Lynn would be able to go back to school.

"Good morning handsome," Angela said walking into his office carrying coffee.

"Hey baby, you're awake early," Derek said, kissing her cheek.

"I couldn't sleep either. Figured we would both need coffee. There has been something on my mind I wanted to talk to you about, too."

Derek slid his chair away from his desk. "I'm all ears, baby."

"How do you feel about Ri seeing a therapist?"

Before Derek could answer, there was a knock at the door. "Hold that thought."

Derek got up and headed to the door, his wife right behind him. When he opened the door, a woman who looked to be in her mid-forties holding a clipboard, smiled back at them. Angela pulled her robe closed over her body and tied it as her husband spoke to the woman.

"How may we help you?"

"Good morning. Are you Mr. Derek Ried?"

"Yes, I am."

"I am Shelly Scott. I'm with social services. Do you have time to talk?"

Derek looked to his wife who nodded. "Of course, please come in."

Angela lead them to the living room where they all took their seats. "What is this about?" Angela asked even though she knew why Mrs. Scott was here.

"I was made aware of the situation with Ri'Lynn and Clayton. First, I want to say that I am sorry to hear about what happened. It has been brought to my attention that you are Ri'Lynn's biological father, correct?"

"Yes, I am."

"But you are no biological relation to Clayton?"

"That's correct. However, we would like him to remain here with us. We will take full responsibilities of both Ri'Lynn and Clayton and are willing to fill out any paperwork needed to do so."

Shelly smiled. "I am so glad to hear it. For older teenagers, putting them in the system doesn't work well for them. It's harder to place them with foster families because of their age. I have all the paperwork you'll need to sign right here."

Shelly presented the paperwork and both Derek and Angela signed them. They talked for a few more minutes before they saw her off. Once she was gone and the door was closed, Derek let out an over dramatic sigh.

"Who was that?" asked Clayton, catching them off guard.

"We didn't know you were awake," admitted Angela.

"That was a caseworker from social services…" Derek started.

"Is she making me leave?" interrupted Clayton.

"No, Clayton, she's not. We signed the paperwork needed to make sure you guys are staying here with us."

"Thank you guys so much. I'm gonna go tell Ri!" Clayton took off to his sister's room.

He knocked and went in. His sister was awake, but still laying in bed. "Ri, we get to stay here! Derek and Angela said they signed all the paperwork."

"Good, I'm so happy Clay," Ri'Lynn said and rolled over.

****

Ri'Lynn sat in the corner of her room reading on her e-reader, taking random looks out of the window. It was three in the morning and everyone in the house and probably the entire town, was asleep. Sleep didn't come easy to her anymore; it was actually nonexistent. Every time she shut her eyes, she could see the image in the mirror no matter how tightly she closed them. She did everything she could to put that horrible experience from her mind, but she wasn't able to, not on her own.

Each time Adam hit her, he broke a little piece off of her. She was doing well to keep herself from shattering, but unsure how much longer she would be able to keep the pieces intact. He made her feel worthless, like her life was literally worth less than anyone else's. He made her feel like her skin color would make people hate her. He made her feel like she deserved to be treated the way he treated her. But worst of all, he took her innocence and she could never get that back.

She knew she should talk to someone. Angela had mentioned to her about talking to a therapist, but Ri'Lynn wasn't sure she could sit in front of a stranger and talk about how she was feeling. But she also knew she couldn't talk to anyone in her family because she didn't want them having to think of her during that; she wanted to spare them the details. Rocking back and forth trying to comfort herself, she got up and headed over to her computer and began to search online for rape victim help. Surprised at how many women used the internet as a way to cope, she got lost in all the different blogs and articles. She even commented on a few and chatted with a few ladies who had been raped themselves.

For the first time in weeks, she felt like she wasn't alone. Logging off her computer, she crawled into bed and laid there thinking. From everything she'd just read, she knew her rape wasn't nearly as bad as others, but it was a horrid experience for her. Excited to wake up in the morning and log back on, she closed her eyes and allowed herself to go to sleep; the deepest sleep she'd gotten in weeks.

Ri'Lynn woke in the morning to the smell of breakfast. Stretching, she slipped on her house shoes and walked sluggishly into the kitchen. Everyone was off to either school or work, but there was a note on the table with her name on it. Yawning, she picked it up and read it.

Food is in the microwave. Just heat it up. Please eat and shower, it'll help you feel better. Then you can get back in bed. Call me if you need anything no matter how small. Love Angela.

She smiled and warmed up the food, keeping the note with her. She loved how loving her family was; she loved being able to call them her family. Taking her food back to her room and closing the door behind her, she logged back onto her computer, website tabs still open. Reading the testimonies of these other ladies really helped and made her want to talk about what happened. Picking up her phone, forgetting she should be in school, she called Lilly. When she didn't answer, Ri'Lynn left her a message telling her she was ready to talk about what happened.

Within five minutes, Lilly called Ri'Lynn back and the two friends talked for hours. Lilly was taking some college classes online and said they could wait because wanted to be there for her best friend. She prepared herself and told Ri'Lynn to tell her as much or as little; whatever she needed. By the end of the phone call, both girls had cried and laughed. Lilly realized how strong of a friend she had and Ri'Lynn was ready to get her life back.

After she hung up with Lilly, Ri'Lynn showered. After her shower, she cleaned her room and opened the windows, letting in the sunlight and fresh air. Feeling like a thousand pounds had been lifted off her shoulders, she climbed into bed for a quick nap; that was the most activity she's done in a month. Before she drifted off, she promised herself tomorrow would be the day she goes back to school and moves on with her life.

The next morning everyone was sitting at the table for breakfast except Ri'Lynn; she hadn't joined them for breakfast even once in the three months they've been staying there. When she ate, she ate in her room alone. Angela was finishing up making Ri'Lynn's plate and was turning around to go take it to her when Ri'Lynn walked in, fully dressed and ready for the day.

"Morning guys," Ri'Lynn chirped, taking the plate from Angela. "Yall look like you've seen a ghost," she smiled and sat down taking a bite of her breakfast.

"We are just glad you've decided to join us on your own this morning," Angela said, smiling.

"I've been doing some thinking. I figured it was time for me to get back to school."

"Wait, are you sure you're ready for that?" questioned Derek, concerned.

"Yes, Dad. I am. I've been online reading some stories from other victims and it really helped. Clayton will be there if I need him. Besides, Adam is locked up so what else could go wrong?"

"I'm really glad they helped, but you can talk to any of us," offered her dad.

"I know I could, but to be honest, I don't want to share those details with you all. I don't want you looking at me differently or treating me any differently. I will talk with you guys if I need it, I promise. But right now I want to focus on getting my life back together."

Pleased and impressed, Derek didn't say anything else. They all talked and enjoyed breakfast together, finally a big happy family again. After breakfast, Ri'Lynn kissed her younger brothers on the head and headed out to the car, Clayton right behind her. He drove them to school, noticing his sister on her phone the entire time.

"Sis, are you sure you're ready for this?" asked Clayton.

"To be honest, I don't think I'll ever be fully ready to go back to school. I mean, it's been three months since your dad has been arrested and we've been living here. I've hardly left my room. I don't want to deal with all the looks people will give me at school. I don't want people to treat me any differently than they used to, but I know they will. Nobody will know how to react or know what to say to me."

"Maybe nobody will know why you were gone," Clayton said hopefully.

"Thanks, but it was all over the news," Ri'Lynn smiled. "It'll be okay. I'll have you and Tommy at school to make things easier."

"Yeah, that's true. Speaking of Tommy…"

Ri'Lynn raised her eyebrows. "Yes? What about Tommy?"

"I think, I'm not for sure, but I think he might be into you. He was pretty worked up almost any time you got hurt by my dad."

"Would it be an issue if he was into me?"

"I mean, I don't think so. It would be a little strange because he's my best friend and all; least I know he would treat you right if y'all got together."

"So you wouldn't mind if I was into him too, right?"

Ri'Lynn didn't give him time to respond. She kissed him on the cheek and jumped out of the Jeep, giggling her way to class. Clayton sat there for a minute, trying to process what had just happened. Did his sister just say she was into his best friend? Smiling and shaking his head, he grabbed his backpack and headed to class. After his first class, he and Tommy always walked to their second class together. He was hoping he would be able to talk to his friend about his sister without making things too awkward.

"What's up bro?" Tommy called out walking up from behind him.

"Shit, just trying to wake up. I hate having math first thing in the morning."

"Right! Who the hell comes up with these schedules?"

They both laughed.

"Hey man, I've been wanting to ask you something," started Clayton. "Don't freak out or anything and be honest with me. Are you into my sister?"

Tommy stopped dead in his tracks. His eyes wide as melons, and Clayton swore he heard his friends heart skip a beat.

"I mean...well, yeah. I've been into your sister for awhile. When I finally grew the balls to tell you, that's when all the abuse started with your dad and I figured it was best to wait. How did you find out?"

"Bro, come on. We've been best friends since diapers. I know when you're into someone."

"You aren't like pissed are you?"

"Nah, I'm not. I mean it'll be a little weird to see y'all start kissing, but I'll just cover my eyes," Clayton laughed as he gave his friend a soft punch on the shoulder.

In Ri'Lynn's afternoon art class, she could feel all the judgemental eyes on her and she tried to ignore them. She wasn't really popular before all this happened, but she wasn't unpopular either. She had friends, but she mostly just hung out with her brother. But since she'd came back, she was the talk of the school; everyone had something to say to her, most of which was nice. Except for the slick comments Billy would say under his breath.

"That's enough, Billy. One more of your rude comments and you'll be heading to the principal's office," their teacher warned.

Ri'Lynn then smarted off a slick comment of her own, making the entire class laugh. Billy's face turned bright red. Redirecting the class, Mrs. Jacobs gave the homework assignment right before the bell. Ri'Lynn grabbed her stuff and was the first one out of the class.

"Hey Ri'Lynn," Billy yelled.

Ri'Lynn kept walking.

"Don't walk away from me, girl."

Ri'Lynn kept walking.

Billy caught up to her and grabbed her arm, forcing her to stop. "That wasn't cool what you did, man. Nobody makes fun of me!"

"Oh, I'm sorry, Billy. I forgot you were the one who had something traumatic happen to you and on your first day back I was making slick jokes about it under my breath. Next time, I'll be a little more considerate," Ri'Lynn mocked shaking, snatching her arm from his grip and walking away, tired of feeling afraid.

Billy, fists balled, followed her as he continued saying more mean things. She turned to him and yelled "leave me alone" in his face, which only pissed him off more. He pushed her face first against the lockers, pressing his body against hers. He was yelling something in her face, but she couldn't hear him; all she could think about was Adam. She could feel her lips begging him to stop, but didn't know if any words escaped her mouth.

Tommy and Clayton just walked out of class into the hall when they heard the commotion. Both boys saw what was happening and their vision turned red. Clayton sprinted right to Billy, punched him in the face and knocked him to the ground. Once Billy let go of Ri'Lynn, she dropped to her knees, Tommy was right there to pick her up; she clung onto him and cried into his arms. He made sure she was stable before he tried to pull Clayton off of Billy, but to no avail. The gym teacher and Mrs. Jacobs had already seen the fight. Once they broke up the boys, they were both sent to the principal's office, everyone went to their last class except for Ri'Lynn and Tommy.

"Mrs. Davis, can I talk to you first?" Ri'Lynn asked grabbing the principal's attention.

"Make it quick," said Mrs. Davis.

"I know you are gonna have to do something about them fighting, but please don't expel them. Billy was making many rude comments to me in Mrs. Jacobs class and I made a comment that made him mad and I shouldn't have done that. After class he confronted me and pushed me against the lockers. Clayton was just trying to protect me."

"I understand that, Ri'Lynn, but who's going to protect Billy from bullies?"

"Billy is the bully!"

"I bet he won't say the same. I just have to be fair here, Ri'Lynn. I understand what you went through was traumatic and I'm sorry that happened to you, but I can't allow your brother to beat up anyone that says something mean to you. If you couldn't handle the rude comments students might say, maybe you should have stayed home longer."

"He doesn't beat up people who say mean things, he only hit Billy because he had me pinned against the lockers and wouldn't let me go. But I guess saying mean things to a girl who just came back from a traumatic event is acceptable in your eyes. And you're right, I should have known students were gonna say mean things and it would be my fault for coming back too soon," Ri'Lynn stormed out of the office, letting the door slam against the wall.

"Meet me at the Jeep once you get expelled," she said as she stormed past her brother.

"Hey, slow down," yelled Tommy as he ran after her.

"Sorry, I'm just so pissed off. Clayton is gonna get expelled because of me," she said.

"I don't think he will get expelled, maybe suspended. But it's not your fault. Billy shouldn't have put his hands on you. It's about time for you to catch a damn break."

"Tell me about it. It's like I'm a damn magnet for bad shit to keep happening," Ri'Lynn said, hanging her head and crying.

"It will pass, storms don't last forever."

"Yeah you're right, but If I wasn't here, you guys wouldn't be in this storm. You both wouldn't have to keep coming to my rescue."

Tommy wiped the tears from her cheek. "Coming to your rescue is something we both love doing. Clayton is a protective big brother and nothing will change that."

"What's your excuse?" She teased leaning closer to him.

Tommy swallowed hard. "I don't like seeing you hurt either."

"Tommy, you are the nicest guy. I've never even seen you fight anyone."

"That's because your brother always beats me to it."

Ri'Lynn leaned in and kissed him on the cheek. "Thank you for always being there for me and my brother."

She opened the trunk of the Jeep and sat down inside, swinging her legs back and forth. Tommy joined her and they sat waiting on Clayton to hear about his punishment.

"You two should have gone to class," Clayton startled them, Tommy reacted and was quickly on his feet in full defense. "Relax man, it's just me."

"I knew that," Tommy tried to play it off. "So what did they say?"

"She gave me this big ole speech about not reacting with my fists everytime Ri'Lynn is in trouble. I told her if she can control her students, I wouldn't have too. She suspended me for two days. I think he got two days for harassing Ri."

"I'm sorry, bub."

"Hey, don't be. That jackass should never opened his mouth let alone pinned you down like that. Are you okay?" he asked picking up her arm and looking over his sister.

"I'm fine," she announced pulling her arm back. "I gave Mrs. Davis an earful too about controlling her students. This school gets on my nerves always trying to make the victims into bullies. I cannot wait until we graduate and get the hell out of here."

A LITTLE HAPPINESS

The two best friends still hang out all the time like they did before life flipped upside down. Clayton was so thankful for Derek for not only taking him and Ri'Lynn in, but allowing his best friend to come over all the time. Tommy had been talking, but Clayton wasn't listening because he was too busy lost in being thankful for his new life.

"Bro, can I ask you something?" Tommy asked.

"What's up?'

"Would you mind if I took Ri'Lynn on a date?"

"Bro, I'm surprised you haven't asked her yet?"

"I've been too nervous," admitted Tommy.

"Ah man, don't be. She's into you, too."

"You think so?"

"I do."

Tommy couldn't believe Ri'Lynn was into him. He didn't want to just text her, so he walked down to her room. He loved coming over to Derek's to see them. The house was filled with so much love; unlike their last home. Once he made it to her room, he stood outside her door for a good three minutes before he knocked softly.

"It's open," Ri'Lynn called from inside. "Hey Tommy, what's up?"

He smiled, "Hey Ri', I was wondering if you'd like to go to dinner and a movie with me this weekend?"

Ri'Lynn jumped up and kissed him on the cheek. "I thought you'd never ask. I'd love too."

Tommy blushed; he could barely form sentences. Somehow he managed to tell her he'd pick her up at five and stumbled out of her room and back to Clayton's.

"Bro, you good? It looks like you are about to pass out."

"I'm great! She said yes to a date and even kissed me on the cheek!"

"Gross. I told you she was into you," Clayton said as he rolled his eyes.

"I can't believe it, honestly."

"Just promise me one thing."

"Sure, anything."

"If you and my sister start dating, I don't want to hear about anything sexual you guys decide to do. If it was anyone else, we could talk about it like we normally do, but not my sister."

"Promise. I didn't plan on talking to you about anything like that," Tommy laughed nervously.

"And one more thing."

"I'm listening."

"If you break her heart, I'll kick your ass."

****

"I had a really nice time with you tonight, Tommy. It wasn't weird or anything," Ri'Lynn admitted, breaking the silence as they sat in the car in the driveway.

"Did you expect it to be weird?"

"I didn't, but with you being my brothers best friend, I didn't know. Can you promise me something though?"

Afraid of what she wanted him to promise, he took a deep breath and asked, "What's that?"

"When we end up dating, and if anything happens and we break up please don't stop being my brother's best friend."

That was easy enough. Tommy took her hand and kissed it. "I promise."

Ri'Lynn leaned over and kissed Tommy. She was shocked at how great of a kisser he was.

"So does this mean you'll be my girlfriend?" Tommy asked.

"You tell me," Ri'Lynn said as she slid out of the car and ran inside.

"How was it?" Her dad asked when she came in the door.

"It was great, Dad."

"I'm glad. He seems like a good kid. You deserve some happiness in your life now anyway."

Ri'Lynn rushed off to her room, smiling from ear to ear. A year ago, if anyone would have asked her if she thought her life would be where it's at now, she would have told them they were crazy. She couldn't have dreamed her life would be like this. Laying down on her bed, she pulled out her phone and had a message from Tommy telling her goodnight. For the first time in a very long time Ri'Lynn was able to go to bed completely happy.

****

Ri'Lynn sat under the tree with a book, reading and watching all three of her brothers and Tommy play basketball. She loved how great they all got along and how close her younger brothers were getting along with Clayton. That had been one of her biggest worries when she first learned who her biological dad was. She didn't want Clayton to feel like he wasn't her brother anymore.

"Hey babe," Tommy said, running up to her.

"Hey, good game out there. My brothers kicked your ass."

"In my defense, they are ruthless, okay?"

They both laughed. Tommy joined her under the tree while the other three kept playing ball. Finally, after the boys were finished playing, they sat down and ate the picnic lunch Ri'Lynn had made for them. It was the perfect Sunday.

ADAM'S FOOL PROOF PLAN

It's been months; five maybe six. Or has it been longer? Adam already lost track of the months he's been locked up. How ever many days, weeks, or months it's been, he's spent every single moment hating Ri'Lynn. As adolescent as that seemed, she took his son from him. Ri'Lynn was just like her mother always causing trouble, but she turned Clayton against him and that was absolutely unforgivable.

Prison wasn't as bad as they made it seem on TV. It wasn't glamorous either, but Adam kept to himself. He didn't plan on causing any issues. He just watched everything that went on trying to figure things out. There was no way he was going to stay here for the ten years he'd been sentenced. His lawyer did say he could possibly get out sooner on good behavior, but he didn't seem too sure on how soon. Not an option for Adam either.

He needed to find a way out of here no matter how hard it could be. He'd been watching the guards and although most of them seemed to be by the book, Adam noticed a couple that looked as if they could be bought. However, he needed to be sure before he could fully get his escape plan together.

"Whatcha' thinking about there, celly?" asked his cellmate.

"Wondering why they call you Rat," Adam answered, eyes scanning through the general population.

"Aw man, that's easy. I used to rat people out to the cops."

"Why?"

"Being a CI pays really good, man."

"Then how did you end up in here?"

"Someone ratted on me."

Adam laughed. "Yeah, that's bound to happen. How long are you in for?"

"I've done five years of a twenty-five year sentence."

"Damn, I couldn't imagine being in here that many years. I've got ten and I can't be here that long."

"Ah, I don't mind. Most of my family is gone and I have way too many enemies. I can help you get out though, if that's what you really want."

For the first time during this conversation, Adam turned and looked at Rat face to face. For the rest of the night, the two cell mates bonded over making a fool proof plan. They had a good six to seven different ways to escape, but Adam wanted one that was flawless; he couldn't get caught trying to get out.

****

Another five months had gone by and the two cellmates had the escape plan narrowed down to two options.

"You're gonna have to die," Rat said suddenly.

"Excuse me?" Adam's body tightened.

"Relax man. I'm talking about your escape. That'll be your best option. I've got a cousin on the outside that can help, but you'll have to pay pretty good; he's got a kid brother he takes care of."

"How much are we talking?"

"He comes to visit every Thursday; that's how he does jobs for people on the inside. I'll talk with him tomorrow when he comes and I can let you know."

"Cool, tell him I'll pay whatever his rate is. I'm ready to get this shit on the ball."

Adam lay awake in bed that night, too excited to sleep. He couldn't believe he was getting closer and closer to the day be could exact his revenge on Ri'Lynn and get his son back. He hoped Rat's cousin would really come through for him because he needed him if this was to go as planned. He trusted Rat as much as he could trust a man with that name, but he hoped his word was as good as him snitching on others. Adam closed his eyes and thought about the day he would be reunited with his son.

The next day, Adam was in his cell doing sit ups. It was visitation time and he had to keep busy while he waited for Rat to come back. He was anxious to find out what Rat's cousin would say. Money wasn't an issue, Adam would pay whatever the guy wanted. He just wanted to know a price so they could work out a day to make this happen.

"He said he will do it," announced Rat, as he walked back into the cell.

"Did he say how much?"

"Fifteen thousand."

"Fuck, that is a lot."

"You can see if he will go lower, but I doubt it. Not since he's getting the girl and then transporting your body. He wants to meet with you next Thursday to discuss details."

Adam smiled. He was excited he was going to die and get out of prison. Rat told him he'd hook up the doctor in the infirmary to falsify the reports to say he was dead. They just had to make it look like he wouldn't have a chance of living before he made it there. They planned until bedcheck where Adam went to sleep dreaming of what was going to happen when he got out.

****

Adam walked into the visitation room and looked for Rat's cousin, with only the description he gave; it was easy to spot him out. Sitting down in front of the guy with a scar running horizontally under his left eye, Adam looked him over before he talked. Ty couldn't be more than mid to late twenties, if he was even that. Adam started wondering how he got in the life he was wrapped up in.

"Ty, thanks for coming."

"Sure. My cousin said you had a big job and needed someone reliable to make sure it happened. I couldn't pass it up. He told you my price, right?"

"He did."

"Is that going to be a problem?"

"No, it'll be fine. I can get you half up front and the rest when the job is done."

Ty agreed and they began talking details. Adam told him about a cabin he had in the woods where he had some of his money hidden. He also said that is where Ty was to take the girl once he grabbed her.

"Not that it's any of my business, but why are you wanting her kidnapped before you escape?" asked Ty.

"I want her to be scared for awhile before I show up. I want her to know I'm still in prison and not know who is behind it."

"Rat mentioned this is your son's sister," Ty paused waiting for a head nod from Adam before he continued. "Will he be a problem?"

"You'll have to get a little creative and grab her when he's not around. He has a best friend, Tommy, who I can get to keep him away from the cabin."

"Sounds good enough for me."

Adam finished giving Ty everything he needed to know right before the guards said visitation time was over. The two men exchanged good-byes and Adam headed off to his cell, feeling quite accomplished. All he had to worry about was making sure things on the inside went down exactly as they planned it. He wasn't too worried because as crazy as it sounds, he trusted Rat.

Ty drove his old, beat up truck out of the prison parking lot and made the hour drive home. He didn't think Adam would accept his price and would have went down in all honesty, but this would be enough money to take care of him and his younger brother for awhile. They could use the money to fix up their rundown childhood home and move far away from the lives they live now. He just had to pull this off without getting caught.

Walking inside and throwing the truck keys on the counter, he headed to his brother's room.

"I'm home," he announced, entering his room.

"Welcome home," said his brother, Dee. "What's the job now?"

"It's nothing, Dee. Don't worry about it."

"If it's nothing, why do you keep doing them?"

"Because we need to get this house fixed up and get the hell out of here."

"Why do we need to leave here, though?"

"Dee, I know you are holding on to this house because we grew up here and it makes you feel close to mom and dad. But bro, this house is run down and in the middle of nowhere. We just need a fresh start."

"Does a fresh start mean no more odd jobs?"

Ty thought for a moment. He never wanted this life for him and his brother. He didn't like doing these jobs because some of them made him very uncomfortable. But working the normal nine to five didn't do it for them. These odd jobs gave him more money than a regular paycheck ever could. "No more odd jobs, I promise."

****

Tommy was grabbing his backpack and walking to his car when his phone rang showing a number he didn't have saved.

"Hello," he answered.

"Tommy?" asked a raspy, unfamiliar voice on the other end.

"Yeah this is him, who's asking?"

"Don't worry about that. Get in your car and listen to what I have to say."

Tommy looked around scanning the area for whoever could be on the other end of the phone, but did as he was told.

"I need you to do something for me. If you do what you're asked, your mom will get the chemo she needs."

"And if I don't do what you ask?"

"Then your mom will die."

The line went dead.

Tommy sat in silence replaying the conversation over and over. Who was this person? How did they get his number? How did they know his mom was sick? More importantly, what did they want him to do? With his questions going unanswered, he drove himself to school, parked and headed quickly to class. He avoids talking to anyone including Clayton and Ri'Lynn. After school he rushed straight home to his mom.

"How was school, honey?" his mom asked like she does everyday.

"It was school. Mom, has anyone been here that you haven't told me about?"

"No, why?"

"Has anyone called you recently about your chemo or anything?"

"No Tommy, nobody's called. What's going on? You're starting to scare me, son."

"I'm sorry mom. It's probably nothing, but just let me know if anyone contacts you, okay?"

He kissed his mom on the forehead and headed to his room. He debated on calling and telling Clayton, but chose to wait because he didn't even know what he was supposed to do yet. Tommy sat on the edge of his bed trying to figure out who that man was and what he wanted. He prayed it wasn't murder or anything, because he would do just about whatever it took to keep his mom alive.

DECOY

For the whole year Adam had been in prison, life went by smoothly; no issues at all. If you asked Ri'Lynn, Clayton, or Tommy life was perfect. Ri'Lynn was just getting out of class. She knew Clayton was waiting at the Jeep for her and Tommy. Stopping by her locker, she switched out her books, grabbed the ones she needed for homework, and headed off to the jeep. Ri'Lynn felt like the walk from the school to the student parking lot was way too long, but stopped complaining when a young girl approached her.

"Excuse me, do you think you could help me?"

"Sure. What do you need help with, hun?"

"I'm trying to get to the library, but I can't remember the directions my grandma gave me."

Ri'Lynn gave her the directions, but the girl still looked confused. "If you'd like, my brother and I could ..."

All of a sudden, someone grabbed Ri'Lynn from behind. She tried to scream but they put something over her face and she could feel her eyes get heavy, her phone fell from her hand. Whoever came up behind her, picked her up and carried her to a van nearby; the young girl following. Once everyone was inside, they sped off.

"Bro, I am starving. I can't wait to grub," Tommy said walking up to the Jeep.

"Me too. Where's Ri'Lynn?"

"She told me to meet her here. Maybe her class is running a 'lil late."

"Maybe. But she still would have said something to me."

"Wanna go to her last class and look for her?" asked Tommy knowing how protective Clayton was of his sister.

Clayton nodded and the two boys went in search of Ri'Lynn. When they had no luck finding her in her last class or around the school, they headed back toward the Jeep. Clayton pulled out his phone to give his sister a call. There was no answer; it rang until voicemail. He hung up and called right back.

"Hold on, I hear something," Tommy said as he stopped them in their tracks. "There," he said and pointed to a phone on the ground.

"It's hers."

Both of them just stood there not too sure what to do next. They scanned the area to see if maybe she was walking around looking for her phone; she wasn't. Tommy suggested they go back to the Jeep in case she was there waiting. Once they made it back to the Jeep and she wasn't there, Clayton called Derek.

"Derek, I think we have a problem."

"Let's not panic just yet," Derek said once the boys got home and explained everything to him.

"Why the hell not?" Clayton pressed. The panic and anger obvious in his voice.

"Watch your tone, young man. She could have gone home with a friend or something. The police will think the same thing."

"I'm sorry, but I don't think you understand. I know she would have told me. Something has happened to her."

"What do you think could have happened, Clayton? Your dad is still in jail and will be for the next ten years; there's no need to panic."

"I don't know, Derek. I really don't. But I can feel something is wrong."

"Okay, tell you what. I'm gonna call and double check with your dad's parole officer. Would that help?"

"It's a start."

Both Clayton and Tommy sat on the couch while Derek made the phone call in his office. Within a few short minutes, he came back rubbing his hands over his head.

"What is it?" Clayton asked as he jumped to his feet.

"Your dad...he was stabbed yesterday morning."

"He was? Is he… did he make it?"

Derek shook his head. "He said there was a big fight at the prison and that they really don't know too much yet. They have to review the footage and do an autopsy. He will call me as soon as he gets any information."

Clayton didn't say anything. He sat back down on the couch and stared at the floor. His dad was dead, why didn't he feel anything? His sister was missing and if he couldn't get her back, he would be left alone to live life with no family. Clayton couldn't feel anything because he was numb, totally and completely, numb. He sat there for hours not realizing both Tommy and Derek were right there with him and they would be just the family he needed.

****

A week had passed since Ri'Lynn's disappearance. The police department organized a couple different search parties. When they found no clues or any evidence she was kidnapped, they called off the search. The chief of police told Clayton and Derek that although he couldn't have his men spend more time looking, he had them on high alert and they would be the first to know. Derek thanked him, but Clayton wasn't as thankful.

"You know that's some bullshit, right?" asked Clayton after Derek saw the police off.

"What is bull shit, Clayton?"

"That he has his men on high alert looking for Ri. He doesn't believe she's even missing. The police think she ran away."

"Can you blame them, son?"

"Ri did not run away!" shouted Clayton.

"Yes, you and I know that. The police don't know her. They are just doing their jobs."

"Do you think this would have happened if my mom was still alive?" Clayton asked in frustration, catching Derek off guard.

"I can't say for sure, son. Why do you ask?" Derek asked, voice soft trying to take Clayton's frustration back down.

"I...I don't know," Clayton tossed his hands in the air. "I just feel like if she was, none of this ever would have happened," he angrily admitted.

"We don't know that for sure, Clayton. Your mom's death was accidental and your dad has always been an abusive person. Who knows what could have happened."

Clayton didn't say anything, but he didn't have to. Derek could see how much this bothered the poor kid. He wanted to talk to him more since he was opening up some, but he had to excuse himself to his office to take a phone call.

Clayton stood in the dining room looking at a map of the town. He was trying to make a plan of where all he wanted to look for his sister. A few of his friends from school and people from the neighborhood said they would help so he wanted to have them cover as much ground as possible. Clayton was so focused he didn't hear Derek come up behind him.

"Clayton. We have a problem," Derek said, making him jump.

"What's going on?"

"That was the prison. They went to do the autopsy on your dad and his body wasn't there."

"What the hell? How?"

"I asked the same thing. They don't know exactly how yet, but they think he somehow faked his own death and escaped."

"Shit," yelled Clayton, slamming his fists on the table. "My dad did it; he took her."

"I hate to say this, but if I find out he had anything to do with this, I'm kicking his pathetic ass," admitted Derek.

They laughed a nervous laugh. Clayton was happy Derek was who he was. He admired how great of a dad he was to Ri'Lynn even though he missed out on most of her life. And he was so good with Brian and Daniel. But the greatest thing about Derek, the thing that gained a lot of Clayton's respect was how he treated his wife.

Clayton had never seen a man love their wife the way Derek loved Angela.

"Why don't you go get your brothers and play video games or something?" asked Derek, breaking up his thoughts.

"My brothers?" questioned Clayton..

"I hope that doesn't bother you that I called them that. I just feel… well I feel like you're family, Clayton. I know I'm not your dad or anything, but Ri'Lynn is my daughter and you're her brother; that makes you my family."

Tears started running down Clayton's face. He ran to Derek who wrapped his arms around him. Derek held him and let him cry. Clayton had been holding it all in and trying to be strong for so long. He was trying to be strong for both him and his sister and to hear those words, they really touched him. Finally, after feeling alone for so long, Clayton felt safe and like he wasn't in this cruel world alone.

"Derek, thank you. That really means a lot to me, man." Clayton said as he wiped away tears.

"I mean it, too. Every word. You wanna go grab Tommy and hangout or something?"

"I'd rather go look for my sister." He said with resolve. His eyes were still puffy but his face stern.

"Okay, well where are we gonna look?"

"Everywhere."

****

Ri'Lynn was in and out of consciousness, but could tell she was moving in some sort of vehicle. She was blindfolded and couldn't even guess where they were taking her. The vehicle turned a lot, so pinpointing what direction they were headed was nearly impossible. Ri'Lynn felt them go from pavement to gravel, she knew that they were headed out of town and that couldn't be good. With nothing more she could do, she laid there praying her brother would find her before she was lost forever.

Finally, after what felt like hours, the car came to a stop. She must have fallen asleep because she could tell she was somewhere new. The smells were different, it was cool, and the ground under her was hard like cement and not cloth-like before. Someone had to have moved her while she was sleeping.

She begged her eyes to open and they did, then they shut soon after; still a little groggy from whatever they put over her nose. She begged her eyes to open again and stay open and this time, she wished she'd kept them shut. What she saw looked like a scene from a horror movie. There were chainsaws, axes, shovels all over the place. She couldn't see what else was around her because it was too dark. Where in the hell was she?

Whatever they gave her to knock her out was fully out of her system now. Ri'Lynn was alert and she did not like what she was seeing. When she stood up to get a better look around, she realized her ankle felt heavy and hurt. She looked down there was a chain around her right ankle; it was on tight which explained why it hurt. Ri'Lynn skimmed the area for a light and noticed a string hanging nearby. She pulled it and looked around as a dim light slowly flooded the room. From the looks of it, she was in some abandoned shed.

As the yellow light spread across the shed, fear spread throughout her body. Ri'Lynn squatted down, she felt very small and helpless like she had many times in the past. She wanted to go home, back to her family and boyfriend. Defeat washed over her and Ri'Lynn curled up in a ball and cried herself to sleep.

Boom.

The noise pulled her awake, heart racing. Ri'Lynn had no idea where she was. Nothing looked familiar to her as she walked forward, one step at a time. Where was she? She was no longer in the shed and... wait. What was that noise she was hearing? It sounded like voices, voices she knew. Following the voices, Ri'Lynn kept going until Tommy and Clayton came into view.

Ri'Lynn opened her mouth to scream at them, nothing came out. No screams, no whisper, no sound at all. She ran like the wind and dashed toward them but abruptly stopped in her tracks as she got closer. She couldn't believe her eyes. Tommy was leaning against his car kissing another girl. Clayton and her two younger brothers were playing basketball. Had they forgotten about her already? Had she been gone that long?

Not going to guess, she walked up to them and spoke. She heard the words come out of her mouth, but nobody else did. Ri'Lynn tried and tried again to get them to hear her, but it was no use. No matter how loud she got, they just couldn't hear her. Hanging her head she just stood there, watching her favorite people be so close but yet so far.

As Ri'Lynn turned to walk away, she heard someone say her name. She spun around to see Brian. He was right in front of her but it was as if he was looking through her, not at her.

"What did you say, Brian?" asked Clayton.

"I said, I thought I heard Ri'Lynn."

"No, you didn't. Ri'Lynn is dead."

Ri'Lynn shot up, sweat rolling down her face. She was in the shed, still chained up to the pole. Relieved it was just a dream, but unnerved because it felt so real. Ready to shake the feeling, and avoiding going back to sleep, Ri'Lynn got up and tried looking for something to get the chain off with.

****

The nightmares happened almost anytime Ri'Lynn closed her eyes. It was getting harder and harder to tell between what was real and what was a dream. The dreams felt so real. They were all different, but in each dream she was either unable to be seen or didn't have a voice. Not too sure why she was dreaming these dreams, she started to wonder if she was going crazy.

Where was she exactly? Who brought her here? How many days has she been here? Five, maybe six or has it been over a week already? Not being able to answer her own questions frustrated her. She could feel the tears coming, but took a deep breath and kept them at bay.

The days ran together and she could tell she was depressed and on the verge of giving up. Seeing how her current situation was, she didn't feel like she had much of a choice but to give up and just wait for whoever was coming for her.

Pull yourself together. You are not this weak minded. Get off your ass and get out of here.

The voice inside Ri'Lynn's head would not shut up. She was glad because it made her want to see how far this stupid chain would let her go. She searched through everything within reach, hoping she could find something to get the chain off with. It looked like nobody had been here in years, maybe even decades. Everything was covered in inches of dust and under that, coats of rust.

She looked around for a door, kicking herself for not doing that first and rushed towards it. Of course, it was locked from the outside and she couldn't escape; not like her chain would allow it anyway. As Ri'Lynn leaned her forehead on the locked door, she could feel a nice, cool breeze. She began to look and see where it came from and came across an old window. The glass was broken, probably from someone trying to break in, and most of the glass was missing. The window was big enough she could fit through it, but she didn't know how far she could get because of the chain.

"There's only one way to find out," she said, out loud to herself and took a step through.

She was able to take a good two steps on the outside of the window before the chain pulled her ankle, preventing any further movement. Her eyes ran across an empty field, nothing for miles but grass and trees. She noticed another, bigger shed off to her left, but it looked just as abandoned. She closed her eyes and slowed her breath to listen. Listened for anything other than the sounds of nature. A car, a train, a construction vehicle; anything other than the chirping birds.

Ri'Lynn dropped to her knees and let out a slight cry. She was in the middle of nowhere and she had no idea how she could get home. She tried to piece it all together. She retraced her steps from class to her locker. Then she remembered she was excited to go eat with her brother and Tommy. On her way to the student parking lot, she helped a little girl…

It was her! She jumped up. *She must have had something to do with this, but why? She's only a little girl.*

Ri'Lynn stood there racking her brain tried hard to remember what happened next and thought about any clues she could have seen but didn't think of. She was so deep in thought she didn't notice the storm clouds roll in around her. All of a sudden, a loud clap of thunder boomed in the sky. Out in the woods, the thunder sounded way different. It felt like it was right over her so she quickly scurried back inside the shed.

The lightning flashed bright, the thunder rumbled loudly, and the rain poured down from the sky; it was beautiful. Ri'Lynn had never been completely away from big buildings or the traffic congestion of city life during a storm. She stood at the window just watching it, taking it all in. Storms didn't usually bother her, but she was slightly nervous about the shed blowing away with her inside.

She laughed at the thought, Ri'Lynn looked around the shed for anything she could cover up with and lay down on. As she was looking, she heard a muffled noise but couldn't figure out where it was coming from. She assumed it was probably a rat and decided not to go looking for it. She spotted an old quilt, she grabbed it and shook it off, in an effort to shake away any possible spiders.

Woof, woof.

"Whoa, a puppy. How did you get in here little fella?" she asked him, squatting down.

She reached out her hand slowly allowing him to sniff her, showing she was no threat. He sniffed her hand for a few minutes then licked her as he jumped up on her leg. She laughed out loud for the first time since she's been here. She picked up the pup and made as comfortable a spot as she could near the post she was tethered to. There was a little shelf she could lean back against and get some rest. Once she was as comfortable as she could get, the dog cuddled in her lap and they fell fast asleep, thunder rumbling off in the distance.

The next morning Ri'Lynn was woken up by kisses from the puppy. She felt like the puppy was obviously abandoned, he was dirty and way too skinny, so she was going to keep him. She couldn't tell what breed or how old he was, she hadn't ever had a dog before. He looked sort of like a wolf so maybe he was some sort of Husky.

"We must give you a name, lil guy," she said and thought for a minute. "How about Little Foot?"

The dog wagged his tail.

"Little Foot it is! Now, let's find something to take this chain off with so we can get out of here."

Little Foot stood to his feet and barked.

She smiled and looked around the shed again for anything that could free her. She tried hitting the chain with random object after random object to no avail. Ri'lynn threw her hands in the air and screamed in frustration, and that's when she saw it. Hanging right there on the wall was a saw. Ri'Lynn tried to get to it but even though the chain would allow her to, her arms were just too short to grab it . She had to try and find something she could use to grab the saw. She was about to grab a metal pole when she heard a truck pull up outside. Her heart skipped a beat; she had no idea what was about to happen. Ri'Lynn quickly hid the pole behind her back and sat down.

After the chain on the front door was removed, in walked a guy who looked to be in his mid to late twenties. He looked like he hadn't slept or showered in weeks.

"I brought you some food," he said as he tossed a bag down on her lap.

"Thank you."

The guy turned to leave.

"Wait, who are you? Why am I here? What do you want with me?" Ri'Lynn pleaded.

"I don't want anything from you, kid. I'm just doing my job. You'll find out soon enough why you're here."

"Where are we?"

"In the middle of bum fuck no where."

He walked out, chained the door, and drove off leaving Ri'Lynn feeling more scared than she did before. Who would want to hurt her? The only person she could think of was Adam, but he's in jail.

"Unless he's not!" she said to Little Foot. "We've gotta get out of here. And fast."

She opened the bag of food the man gave her and ate half of a sandwich and gave the crust to Little Foot. She found her backpack and put the rest of the food in it for later. She grabbed the pole and she hit the chain over and over; nothing happened. She took her shoe and sock off to try to slip her foot out of the shackle but to no avail.

This is not a movie. I am not gonna break my ankle or cut off my foot to escape, but I'm not gonna sit here and wait for Adam to kill me, either.

Finally, she used the pole to grab the saw that caught her eye earlier. After fifteen minutes, she got her foot out of the chain. It hurt like hell and bled a lot, but at least she was free! She ripped part of her shirt sleeve, she wrapped it around her ankle as tight as she could, and put her sock and shoe back on. Ri'Lynn grabbed her backpack, threw all of her books on the table except for one book she wanted to use as a way to mark her trail in case she needed to find her way back to this dreadful shed. After she filled the bag with few things she could use as tools, Ri'Lynn was ready.

Without wasting anymore time, she and Little Foot took off out of the shed. Ri'Lynn's plan was to try and follow the truck's tire tracks, using the books pages to mark her trail. Her ankle hurt so bad and was going to slow her down quite a bit. She wasn't too sure how far she would get, but she had to try and get as far away from here as she could. If Adam was the one who was behind this, he brought her out here to kill her and she wasn't sticking around to let that happen.

Ri'Lynn had been missing for an entire month. Clayton was beside himself. He had no idea what to do without her. He wasn't going to stop looking though. He would never stop looking until she was home. He refused to think the worst, he would keep looking under every rock and in every abandoned house until he brought her home.

Clayton noticed Tommy nodding off in the passenger seat, "Let's call it a night, man," he suggested.

"Are you sure? We can stop and get coffee and I'll be fine," protested Tommy.

"It's cool man, we can get rest and start up again tomorrow. Derek said the cops are still looking everywhere for her as well. Hopefully one of us will find her soon."

"We will," Tommy reassured.

After Clayton dropped him off, Tommy went inside and was heading to his room until he saw is mom asleep in the chair, book on her chest, glasses falling off her face. He grabbed the glasses and book, then gently tried to wake his mom.

"Did you find her?" She asked with a sleepy voice.

"Not yet, Mom."

"You guys will find her. I am so proud of you, son."

"Thanks Mom. Now off to bed."

He kissed her on the forehead and headed off to his room, closed the door behind him. Tears started to escape from his eyes. He couldn't stop thinking about how scared Ri'Lynn must be. Was she hurt? Was she alone?

This school year started out great; he'd finally gotten the girl of his dreams; only to have her taken from him. He was angry because he should have been there to protect her, to keep her safe. Tommy went to bed with a heavy heart and blaming himself.

Back at Derek's, everyone was asleep but Clayton; he hadn't really slept since his sister went missing. The police didn't suspect his dad had anything to do with it, but he was positive his dad was behind this in some way or another. Clayton knew it was the job of the police to find her, but he also knew they didn't know his dad, not like he did. If he wanted to find Ri'Lynn, he had to think like his dad.

Revenge would be the motivation that would be driving his dad, so what would he have planned? Clayton knew his dad would have some sort of plan, he never did anything half-assed. He knew his dad would have planned the actual kidnapping, but did he have it planned out as to where he was keeping her? Did he grab her himself? Or does he have someone helping him? What if Ri'Lynn was dead?

The questions kept coming making Clayton's head spin and his stomach turn. Sleep wasn't coming, so Clayton willed himself out of bed. He had to do something, anything to keep his mind from thinking the worst. He decided to go grab a snack from the kitchen. He rummaged through the fridge, nothing sounds appetizing so he closed the door, revealing a figure standing right behind the door.

"Shit, Daniel. You scared the mess out of me."

"I'm sorry, I didn't mean to."

"It's fine, I just didn't hear you walk up. What are you doing awake?"

Daniel cried silently into his hands.

"Hey, hey. It's okay, bub. Why don't you come back to my room with me?" Clayton wrapped his arms around Daniel and lead him back to his room.

"Tell me whats wrong," said Clayton after they settled in his bed.

"I… I miss Ri'Lynn. I wasn't very nice to her when I first met her. Now I just want my sister back," cried Daniel as he threw himself down on the bed.

Clayton patted him on the back and let him cry for a minute. "Now, now, Daniel. You know, Ri'Lynn would be sad if you were crying."

Daniel sat up. "She would?"

"Yes, she wouldn't want you to be sad. She would want you to stay strong for Brian."

"Why strong for him?"

Clayton pondered his thoughts for a moment. "When you're a big brother, you have to do things to make sure your younger sibling doesn't see you sad. You have to show them how strong you are and that they can always count on you."

"Is that why you haven't stopped looking for Ri?"

"Yup, and I won't stop looking for her either."

"I want to help look, too!"

"Okay, okay calm down. You have to be well rested if you want to help look for her. Why don't you head to bed and when we get up tomorrow you can go with me to look. How does that sound?"

"It sounds perfect. Thanks, Clayton."

Brian jumped off the bed and headed for the door.

"Hey Brian," called Clayton.

"Yeah?"

"You can talk to me any time, about anything, okay?"

Brian smiled. He ran over, hugged Clayton, and ran out of the room. Clayton shook his head and laughed. He climbed under the covers and fell asleep. It was the best sleep he'd had in weeks.

****

Derek, Angela and the boys had been out all morning looking for Ri'Lynn. Several of the people from the town were helping look too. Sitting on a tree stump, Derek hung his head and began to cry. He didn't let anyone see him like this, but he was a mess inside.

Being out in the woods from sunup to sundown and still no sign of Ri'Lynn, broke his heart. His daughter was out there, scared, and there was nothing he could do about it. Would they be able to find her before it was too late?

A stick cracked, he lifted his head to see Clayton standing there.

"Are you okay, Derek?" he asked.

"I'm fine, son," Derek forced a smile and wiped his eyes.

"You know you are a terrible liar. I seen the tears. It's okay to cry."

"It is okay to cry, but I'm the dad. I've got to be strong for my family."

"Did you know you can be strong for your family *and* let them be strong for you at the same time?"

"I...uh. I guess I didn't think about that, Clayton."

Clayton placed a hand on Derek's shoulder and gave it a firm squeeze. "You can lean on us, too. If you use all your energy hiding your feelings, we won't be able to help keep you from falling apart. And if you fall apart, who will keep the rest of us together?"

Derek sat there, mouth agape. Clayton smiled and walked away as Angela walked up. She stood in front of her husband as he wrapped his arms around her, placing his head on her stomach. She ran a hand down the back of his neck.

"You okay, baby?"

"I am," Derek leaned back so he could see his wife's face. "Did you hear any of that?"

"I sure did. He's right, you know?"

"I know he is. I just can't believe he is that wise at his age."

"He's gone through a lot. Wisdom was sure to come. Do you want to talk about it?"

Derek stood and stretched, then hugged his wife and whispered, "I'm afraid I won't have the chance to be a real father to Ri'Lynn. I'm scared that whoever took her, will kill her before I get the chance to show her how a dad is supposed to love his daughter."

A RANDOM SURPRISE

Since his daughter has been missing for three whole months, Derek's been working from home—when he's decided to work. He hasn't been getting much work done because he's been looking for her. Making sure his boys went to school even though they begged him to help look for her was a struggle every single day. However, Derek didn't fight Clayton on going to school; he knew it was a lost cause.

A knock on the front door summoned him from his office. When he opened the door, he was in shock by the ghost who stood in his entryway.

"Holy shit…" was all he managed to say.

"Mom?" Clayton questioned as he walked up behind Derek, mouth agape.

"I hope I'm not bothering you by stopping by."

"Bothered? No, but consider me surprised since people don't come back from the dead," Derek admitted, stepping aside. "Please, come in."

They migrated to the living room where they sat in silence, nobody wanted to address the elephant in the room. Clayton sat next to Derek, leg bouncing rapidly. He looked at his mom and he couldn't help but feel angry. How was she alive? Why was she here? Clayon couldn't handle this and got up and walked out of the room.

"Clayon, please don't go," Ruby called after him.

"Let him go," Derek said. "He's pretty upset. Just give him a minute."

Derek excused himself and went after Clayton and took a seat next to him on his bed. Clayton's body was tense and he was staring at the floor. Derek placed his hand on his shoulder and gave him a squeeze.

"Want to talk about it, son?" Derek asked.

"Not really," started Clayton. "But how could she? How could she do this? How is she alive? How come she hasn't been to see me before?"

"I honestly have no idea. We could go talk to her and you can ask."

Clayton got up and kicked the edge of his bed. "I don't want to talk to her."

Derek waited a minute before he said, "I know you don't, but if you don't talk with her, you might never get the answers you want."

Clayton thought for a minute and hugged Derek. "Thank you."

"Anytime, kid. Now let's go get you some answers."

They walked back into the living room to a Ruby who was sitting on the couch, waiting. Clayton sat on the edge of the couch and rubbed his hand across his face. He couldn't even look at his mom. He didn't want to talk to her at all, but Derek was right. If he wanted to get any answers he had to.

"Mom, I thought… we thought you were dead," Clayton said, eyes never leaving the floor.

"I know, son, and that's how it needed to be."

Clayton raised his head and narrowed his eyes. "Excuse me? You needed your children to think you were dead for ten years? You needed them to feel abandoned and lost?"

"Clayton, please. You don't understand…"

"You're damn right I don't understand," Clayton yelled, standing to his feet.

"Boy, watch your mouth in front of your mother," warned Derek as he stood and placed his hand on Clayton's shoulder. Derek turned to Ruby,his voice was a little more hostile. "Ruby, you can't blame him. You did just randomly show up. Care to explain yourself more?"

Ruby shook her head yes, she looked around. "Where's Ri'Lynn? I want her to hear this too."

Derek and Clayton exchanged glances before Derek said, "Ri'Lynn is missing."

"Missing? What do you mean missing?"

"He means missing! She's been kidnapped. Taken. Gone," spat Clayton.

"I can't believe this," she yelled and stood to pace the room. "You were supposed to project her. How could you let this happen?" she screamed, pointing in Derek's face.

"Mom, stop. It's not his fault. Derek is a great dad to Ri'Lynn. She's lucky to have a dad like him. He's one of the greatest guys I know. If you are gonna get mad at anyone, get mad at me. I should have been there to protect her. I shouldn't have ever left her alone."

Clayton tried to keep it together but he broke down and cried. His mom tried to comfort him, but he just pushed her away. Derek went and sat next to him and Clayton instantly fell into his arms. Derek put one arm around him and looked at Ruby with apologic eyes.

"Son, it's not your fault. You are a great big brother to your sister and take good care of her. Nobody knew your dad was out. We were all living with ease and not alert. Don't beat yourself up. Your sister needs you to help find her," Derek told him.

"Wait, is Adam out of jail?" questioned Ruby.

"Yes, he is. Apparently he escaped around the same time Ri'Lynn went missing."

"And the police think he could be behind Ri'Lynn being missing?"

"They haven't exactly said that. Clayton and I feel like it's definitely possible."

"So, what have the police said exactly? Are they making any headway with finding out where Ri'Lynn is being held?"

"They aren't telling me much," admitted Derek.

"I figured with a kid missing, there would be cops all over your house."

"There was when she went missing. We have a patrol car stationed here at night and another one that drives through the neighborhood every hour."

"Shouldn't they have someone here in case Adam tries to call with a randsome?"

"They have our lines tapped. If it was him, they don't think he wants any kind of ransom."

"They don't? Well what do they think he wants then?"

"Revenge," Derek admitted. "But now it's time for you to give Clayton the answers he deserves."

Ruby took a deep breath, "After the accident, I was ready to lay there and just give up. I didn't have any fight left in me. I was barely holding on by the time I got to the hospital. They had told me you kids were fine and I knew your dad would take good care of you both, so I accepted the offer that was given to me."

"What offer, Mom?"

"Sister Mary Catherine came to visit me. She sat with me for days in the hospital while I recovered. Once I was well enough to comprehend what she was saying, she offered for me to come back with her to her nunnery to get well. She had informed me that everyone thought I was dead and I could finally be able to get out from under Adam's thumb. I worked real hard to get my strength back both mentally and physically so I could leave and get my life back; get my kids back."

"Wait, so you thought you would just stay there all these years and then just stroll back into our lives and everything would go back to normal?"

"Not exactly back to normal. I figured I'd be able to take you and your sister and start a new life together somewhere else far away from your dad."

"I can't believe you are serious right now. You've been 'dead' for ten years and you think you're just gonna come back into our lives like that? Mom, you're practically a stranger. And a criminal for faking your own death."

"How did you know the kids were with me? And how did you know where I lived?" asked Derek.

Ruby bit on her nail like she always did when she was nervous. She pulled her finger from her mouth and told them she had the sisters keeping an eye on her kids. They informed her of Adam's arrest and kept her in the loop of where the kids got placed. She expressed her shock when she learned they were staying here with Derek.

The front door opened and in walked Angela whose eyes grew at the sight of Ruby.

"Hello, I didn't know we were having company or I would have brought more for lunch."

"It's no problem, I stopped by unannounced. I'm Ruby, Clayton and Ri'Lynn's mom," she said, extending her hand.

Taken aback, Angela shot a look to Derek before she responded as she took the food to the kitchen. "Nice to meet you, Ruby. I'm Angela, Derek's wife."

Derek excused himself and followed his wife. "Baby, I'm sorry I didn't call you and tell you. There was a knock at the door and when I opened it, she was standing right there."

"It's okay, love. I saw Clayton wiping his eyes. Is he okay?"

"Aside from learning his mother has been alive for the last ten years and living with nuns, he broke down about his sister. He blames himself. Poor guy is trying to be so strong."

"Wait, she's been living where?" Angela laughed uncontrollably.

"Baby, hush before she hears you."

"You're right. I'm sorry." Angela pulled herself together and back to being serious. "Clayton is a really good kid. I hope our boys grow up to be close like those two."

"Yeah, me too."

Back in the living room, Clayton couldn't help but feel angry when he looked at his mom. How could she have done this to them? How could she just show up like this after all these years? Did she honestly think this was the best decision? Why didn't she try to reach out sooner and let them know she was alive?

"Son, you look upset."

"I am, Mom. It's been ten years. We've been without you for ten whole years."

"That's exactly why I thought you'd be happy to have me back."

"Mom, I thought you were dead! I didn't expect to get you back."

"Then why are you mad I'm alive?"

Clayton thought for a minute. "I wouldn't say I'm mad you're alive. I am pissed off because you've been alive and hadn't cared enough about us to come back sooner. I'm pissed off because dad was beating Ri'Lynn. He raped her. And I was trying to protect her and keep her safe while living my own life. I needed help. I needed my mom. Ri needed you, too."

"I… I don't know what to say to that. I'm sorry, Clayton. If I would have known you felt this strongly, I never would have stopped by."

"How did you expect me to feel? You couldn't have thought I'd run and jump into your arms, did you?"

"Well no, not exactly."

"Honestly, you wouldn't have known how I'd feel because you don't know *me.* I'm nineteen. I'm much different than that eight year old boy you once knew."

Ruby didn't say anything. She just got up and ran out of the house, tears streaming down her face. Clayton sat there, expressionless. He didn't mean to be so harsh to his mom, but he was mad at her. Maybe after he found Ri'Lynn and she was home he could work on forgiving his mom. Until then, all his focus and energy needed to be on finding his sister. He got up and walked into the kitchen and informed Derek and Angela that his mother had left.

They all grabbed a plate and sat and talked. They enjoyed lunch and the conversation, making sure not to talk about Ruby. After lunch, Clayton cleaned up while Angela kissed her husband goodbye and headed back to work. Clayton headed to his room so he could be alone because today was just too much to handle for him.

****

Ruby sped back to the nunnery. The words her son said stung more than she wanted. She didn't know what to expect when she showed up at Derek's but she hoped it would go better than this. Once back at the nunnery, she walked right to her room hoping Sister Mary Cathrine didn't see her. Unfortunately, she didn't go unnoticed because there was a knock at her door.

"Ruby, care to talk about it?" asked Sister Mary Cathrine when she came in the room.

"Sister, it was horrible. My son hates me and my daughter is missing. I should have listened to you and stayed 'dead'."

"I'm sure your son doesn't hate you. He just needs time. He's probably dealing with a lot of stress worrying about his missing sister."

"You're right."

"Give it time, Ruby. He knows you're alive and where you're staying. He will come to you when he's ready."

"What if he never comes, Sister?"

"Then you go on with your life. Ruby, you knew this was a possibility when you came here ten years ago. You have to accept whatever the outcome is."

Ruby knew how much truth Sister Mary Cathrine's words held. Ten years ago, coming here felt like the perfect solution to her problems; it felt right. Now, not so much. Unable to figure out what would happen next, Ruby turned on some music and continued working on her knitting project for the rest of the night, and tried hard to forget about the day she'd just had.

LOST IN THE WOODS

Ri'Lynn has been walking for what seemed like hours and is still no closer to finding a way out of these woods or any sign of human life. Unsure if she was walking in circles or if she was actually headed in the right direction, she sat down to rest her foot. Little Foot curled up next to her, and closed his eyes.

Maybe I should find us a place to sleep for the night. We've been walking for hours and could use the rest.

She wished they still had the shelter from the shed, but refused to backtrack to find it. Ri'Lynn got up and looked around for a place for them to sleep. She didn't hope to find much of a shelter in the woods but then she came across a huge Weeping Willow tree. It was full with branches so long they touched the ground. She parted the branches to the side and slid inside the tree. The inside was open enough she could squat without hitting her head on any low branches. Ri'Lynn looked through the branches and couldn't see much of the outside world.

This is perfect.

Ri'lynn placed her things under the bows of the tree and scooped up Little Foot to go look for some sort of food to eat. With no water in site, she quickly ruled out fishing as an option. Besides some blueberries, most of what Ri'Lynn found looked to be poisonous. She had to resort to eating what she didn't want to: crickets, grasshoppers, ants, and earthworms.

The taste didn't bother her too much, especially when she didn't have anything else. Her brother made her try insects when she was younger so she knew what they would taste like. It started to get dark and she took her finds back to the Weeping Willow. She did her best to imagine she was eating some of her favorite foods rather than creepy crawlers and laughed out loud at the thought of a cricket tasting like a cheeseburger. Little Foot had already curled up in a ball and gone to sleep.

Ry'lynn ate one last cricket then put the rest in her backpack to save for later and made herself as comfortable as she could. Sleeping on the Earth's hard ground didn't bother her. No, it was her swollen, throbbing ankle that made sleep evade her. Thoughts of her family began to creep into her mind. Ri'Lynn wished she could be back home with her family. She missed her brother so much and wished he was here because he would love sleeping in a tree and eating crickets.

Her laughter turned into tears as she realized exactly how alone she was. She felt so lonely it hurt. Ri'Lynn was more afraid of running into a bear or bobcat than she was worried about stumbling across Adam. She pushed the thoughts of him out of her mind, closed her eyes and willed sleep to come. She finally fell into a deep sleep, she slept the entire next day, too.

Ri'Lynn was fully rested, but her ankle was getting worse. She decided she would walk just a little longer and then would stop for a break and a snack. She didn't want to push herself too much. Little Foot looked tired, too. As she pushed a little further, she saw a house. She blinked repeatedly and rubbed her eyes to make sure her mind wasn't playing tricks on her. It wasn't, the house was real.

She limped up the broken steps of the rundown house and knocked on the door praying someone was home. Within a few minutes, her prayers were answered as the door opened and in front of her stood a tall, athletically built, very attractive, young guy. He looked to be in his early to mid 20s, with his hair pulled back into a bun on his head. He had carmel skin and the way the sun caught his eyes, made her speechless. He had the most beautiful eyes.

"Hey there, sweetheart. Are you lost?" he asked, pulling Ri'Lynn from her thoughts.

"I kind of am. Is there any way I could borrow your phone to call my brother?" Ri'Lynn asked shifting her weight off her hurt ankle.

"Are you hurt?"

"It's just my ankle. I'll be okay."

"Why don't you let me take a look at that?" he asked.

"Can Little Foot come in, too?" asked Ri'Lynn as she pointed to her dog.

"Of course. That little guy looks hungry."

Ri'Lynn followed the guy inside, praying he wasn't a serial killer but didn't have the energy to figure out first. There had to be a rule about serial killers not being attractive, right? She looked around the house as he leads her to the living room. It was extremely out of date and looked like it needed a lot of work done to it. There were holes in the floor, the walls, and ceiling. It was kind of messy, too. She wondered if he lived here alone or where his parents were.

He had her sit down on the couch and headed for the kitchen. He quickly came back with a sandwich, chips, pop, and even some food for Little Foot, too. After he placed the food on the ground for the dog, he disappeared again, this time reappearing with a first aid kit.

"I'm no expert, but I can clean that ankle up so it doesn't get infected."

Ri'Lynn didn't object. He gently took off her shoe, her sock, and then rolled up her pant leg to mid calf. He cleaned off her ankle and apologized when she winced in pain. After all the dirt was cleaned off of it, he applied some antibiotic and wrapped it up all nice.

"Thank you so much. It feels so much better already. I'm Ri'Lynn, by the way."

"I'm glad I could help. You can call me Dee."

"Thank you, Dee."

He smiled. "What were you doing way out here anyway?"

"You wouldn't believe me if I told you."

"Try me," pressed Dee, eyebrows raised.

Ri'Lynn wasn't sure if she should tell him or not because she didn't know if she could trust him. She also didn't know if he had anything to do with her being out here. Figuring she had nothing to lose, she told him.

"I was abducted at my school and when I woke up, I was in some shed in the woods with a chain around my ankle."

Dee's body got tense. He ran to the window. "Shit, he's home."

"Who's home?"

Dee didn't answer her, but picked her up and carried her down the hall into a bedroom, Little Foot right behind. He opened his closet, pushed some clothes out of the way and hit the wall. A piece of the wall fell out and he told her and Little Foot to get inside.

"Dee, what is going on?" Ri'Lynn asked with scared eyes.

"My brother is home."

He didn't wait for her to respond. He quickly put the piece of the wall back and pushed the clothes to cover it. He shut his closet door and ran to grab the first aid kit. He was able to put it away before his brother walked in the door.

"What do we have to eat, Dee? I'm starving," asked his brother as he sat down on the couch. "What are you, a slob? Pick up your dishes, ass."

"Sorry, I forgot. So, how was your day?" questioned Dee nonchalantly.

"It was okay. I'm trying to finish this job so I can get away from this dude. He's nuts, but the pay will be good enough to get us out of this dump and far away from here."

"I don't mind it."

"Not all of us are like you, little brother."

"What does that even mean?"

"Dee, our house is shitty. We live in the middle of nowhere and you have no friends."

Dee knew that all too well and decided not to get into it again with his brother about the house like they've done so many times before. This was the house he grew up in. It was their parent's house and he didn't want to ever leave because he felt like he would be leaving them. He quickly changed the subject. “What's the job,Tyler?”

“Why do you care? You've never been interested in my jobs before.”

“I dunno, I was just curious.”

“I had to kidnap this girl and hold her until this guy gets here.”

“Jesus, Ty. What are you thinking?”

“I’m only thinking about the money. We really need the money. Besides, I didn’t hurt her or anything.”

“I know we need the money but money isn’t everything, Ty. You could get in some serious trouble.”

“Only if I get caught. Now shut up about it.”

Dee didn't say another word; he knew Ri'Lynn was the girl his brother kidnapped. Unsure what to do next, he grabbed a couple snacks and went to his room, and locked the door behind him. He opened the closet and told Ri'Lynn to be quiet.

“My brother is the one who took you,” whispered Dee after he turned on the TV.

“Did he say why?”

“He said he was doing a job and this guy was gonna pay him a lot of money.”

“It's gotta be Adam, my step dad,” Ri'Lynn admitted to herself as she sat down on his bed.

“Why would your stepdad want you kidnapped?”

“He was real abusive to me and after he raped me, he got sent to prison. He must have gotten out or is planning an escape. I’m sure he wants revenge.”

Dee put his hand on her leg. “I’m sorry that happened to you. I don't know how anyone would want to hurt the ones they love.”

She smiled and shifted, changing the subject. “So where are your parents?”

“They died in a car accident when I was twelve.”

“I'm so sorry, Dee.”

“It's okay. I mean it sucks because I miss them both so much. We don’t have any other family either. It's just me and my brother now.”

There was a knock on the door that made them both jump.

"Dee, who you talking to in there?"

"Nobody, Ty," he yelled as Ri'Lynn scurried back in the closet.

"Open the door man. What are you doin', jacking off?"

"No, I'm not jacking off," Dee said as he opened the door. "I was just watching TV."

"With the door locked?"

"Ty, I'm grown. If I want to lock my door, I can."

"You're right, you're right. But I feel like you're hiding something."

"I'm not," Dee lied.

"If I find out you are…"

Dee pushed him out of his room and shut the door in his brothers face, and locked it. He took a deep breath and leaned his head back on the door. He had no idea what he was going to do, but he needed to get this girl out of here before his brother found out she was here. Or worse, before her step dad realized she was missing. He didn't know what kind of person that guy was, but he couldn't be a good one if he would pay someone to kidnap his step daughter for revenge.

OUT OF OPTIONS

Two weeks had gone by since Ri'Lynn knocked on Dee's door. Pride flooded over her after she had made it out of the shed, through the woods for however many days, and onto the front porch of this house that should have been torn down ages ago. It was just her luck to knock on the door of the guy who kidnapped her. As her and Little Foot were cramped in this weird hideout in Dee's closet, all that pride was gone and she felt entirely defeated. This was not what she had in mind when she escaped.

She wanted nothing more than to be home with her family and in her comfortable bed, and a nice, hot shower. However, Dee was great. He took her in, cleaned her ankle, let her wash up a little and has lied to his brother about her. She felt sorry for them, living the way they lived; no phones, no internet, no nice things.

Dee had made silly plan after plan to try and sneak her out, but none of them worked; his brother always got in the way. Ri'Lynn felt weird being here with Dee, a good weird though. She couldn't explain why she felt what she felt, but maybe it was because she had spent so much time alone and needed human companionship. Whatever the case, she hoped after all this was over, her and Dee could remain friends.

"The coast is clear, you can come out now," Dee summoned her from the closet.

"Why are you still doing this?" Asked Ri'Lynn as she climbed onto his bed.

"Doing what?"

"Helping me? I know you don't like lying to your brother."

"Ah, I don't like lying to him. But I...I don't know. I feel it's only right to help you since he's the one who grabbed you."

"Won't you be upset if he finds me and gets mad at you?"

"Nah, he'll be fine. Even if he does find out, he'll get over it. Besides, I got to know you and Little Foot. I think it's been worth it."

Ri'Lynn blushed. He was so sincere and genuine. She had really grown to like him in these two weeks.

"You're a great guy, Dee."

"Thank you. Just so you know, my brother is a great guy, too. He just got caught up trying to make us some money. After our parents died, it was up to him to take care of us. He wants to fix this house up and sell it. Then move far away from here."

"But you don't?"

“No, I don’t. I mean I would love to fix it up, but this is the last thing I have left of my parents. I grew up in this house. It’s not just any house, it’s my home.”

****

Every time Dee tried to sneak Ri’Lynn out, his brother would come around and mess up their plan. And since they shared a phone that Ty always had, there was no way for them to call her brother. See hate lying to his brother and was afraid they would get caught, he really enjoyed having Ri’Lynn around. He hadn’t had any friends in awhile and never had anyone over. He was too embarrassed of how his house looked to ever invite anyone over. Thankfully she didn’t seem to mind.

“We've gotta get you out of here,” Dee said.

“How are we going to do that? We haven’t had much luck,” laughed Ri’Lynn.

“I don't know. Maybe I can use your dog. Tell him I was working in the yard when I saw him and say that I want to keep him. I could say I would need to use the truck so I could go into town and get some dog food. You can sneak out the back while I ask him and get in his truck.”

"Do you think that will work?"

"It's worth a shot. We can try first thing in the morning. And then I'll take you straight home."

Ri'Lynn hugged Dee out of happiness and joy. She didn't know how long she's been missing, but it had to be more than a couple of months by now. The thought of going home made her ecstatic. Dee turned just a smidge and planted a kiss on her lips, a kiss like something she had never felt. Every part of her wanted to keep kissing him, but she pulled back.

"I'm so sorry. I...I didn't mean to," stumbled Dee.

"It's okay. I just have a boyfriend, I think."

"What do you mean, you think?"

"I mean I had one before I got kidnapped. I don't know how long I've been gone; I lost track after three weeks. He could have moved on already. Hell, everyone could have moved on and forgot about me."

"I doubt anyone forgot about you. They are probably out looking for you right now."

Ri'Lynn sat next to Dee as he watched T.V. She didn't watch at all. Her mind worried that she'd been gone so long everyone forgot about her. She wondered if she should even try going back home or if she should just try to start a new life on her own. She decided it was unrealistic for a seventeen-year-old high school junior so she laid her head back against the wall unsure what to do.

Later that night, Dee came and told her she didn't have to hide because his brother was gone on a new job for a couple of days. Disappointed their plan was interrupted again, she was excited to be able to get out of the closet and out of his room for a change. Dee's room was neater than the rest of the house, but she felt like she was going crazy staying locked in that room. However, she was slightly happy their plan to get her home had to be put on hold.

They sat in the living room and watched T.V., laughing and joking around. They ate snacks and then sat on the back porch and watched the sun set. For the first time in months, Ri'Lynn didn't feel scared. She actually enjoyed her time with Dee so much that she started hoping Tommy had moved on and forgotten about her.

Before she could talk some sense into herself, she leaned over and kissed Dee.

Fireworks went off immediately. Maybe not visually, but inside each one of them. Dee pulled her onto his lap, lips never parting from each other's. Her hands were wrapped around his neck pulling him to her. Dee felt his hands slip under her shirt and that's when he stopped himself.

"Ri'Lynn…"

"You don't have to say anything, Dee. I understand," she said as she dismounted lap.

"But I do want to say something. You've been here two weeks and I feel like I've known you forever. I don't know what's going to happen, but I'm really starting to like you. I only stopped because I don't want you cheating on your boyfriend if you still have one."

"I appreciate that, Dee. If I'm being honest, I really like you too. When I'm hiding in your closet, you are the one I'm thinking about. I kind of feel guilty, but at the same time I don't."

"Wouldn't you consider this cheating?"

"I mean, yeah it is. But let's be honest here, I've been gone for months. I can't expect him to wait around on me. What if I can't get home for another year? Or ever?" she questioned, tears running down her face.

"You will get home if it's the last thing I do. I will make sure of it," he said as he wiped her eyes. "Why don't you take a shower? Now that my brother is gone it'll be a good time."

She agreed, embarrassed they made out and she hadn't showered in awhile. Dee got up to grab a t-shirt and a pair of his compression pants. He showed her the bathroom, gave her a towel and washcloth, and left her to shower.

In the bathroom, Ri'Lynn looked at herself in the mirror for the first time since she'd been here. Her hair was a tangled mess, she had dirt all over her body, and a cut on her cheek she didn't know she had. She couldn't believe Dee would let her into his house looking like something from a horror movie. She discovered more bruises as she stripped down, an all too familiar site. She slid into the shower and let the hot water pelt against her back.

After her shower, Dee told her she could sleep in his bed and he would take the couch. She tried to protest but his mind was already made up. She thanked him and lay in the bed with Little Foot snuggled right next to her. The bed was extremely comfortable, or she was just that tired, Ri'Lynn could feel her eyes get heavy. Her last thoughts were wishing Dee was laying next to her.

In the middle of the night, Dee jolted awake to screams coming from his room. Afraid for the worst, he ran to his room looking around for what could have made her scream. When he saw nothing and realized she was just having a nightmare, he turned on the light and waited for it to pass or her to wake up. Suddenly, Ri'Lynn sat up fear, written on her face, gasping for air.

"Ri'lynn it's okay. You were just having a nightmare. You're safe," Dee reassured her.

Her eyes softened as she locked onto him. "Oh good. That was scary."

"What was it about?"

"My step dad."

"Have you been having nightmares this whole time?"

"No, I actually haven't had one in awhile. I used to have them all the time right after it happened. I had a few when I was in the shed, but I guess I haven't really been sleeping since I've been taken. Your bed is so comfy. I guess I was really tired. I'm just glad your brother is still gone."

Dee laughed nervously, "Me too. I don't know how I'd explain that one to him. But you are safe now. You can try to go back to sleep."

"I don't know if I can sleep. I'm too scared to try. Will you stay here with me?"

"Of course I will."

Dee climbed into the bed next to Ri'Lynn. He sat up mostly, leaning back on the wall, arms behind his head. Once he was settled, Ri'Lynn scooted toward him and laid her head on his lap. Keeping one arm behind his head, he used his other to run his fingers through her hair hoping to help her fall back asleep. Her breathing started to go back to normal and he could tell she was falling back to sleep. He planned to wait until she was fully asleep before he would move back to the couch; except he fell asleep before he could move.

The next morning, Ri'Lynn woke to the sound of birds chirping, the sun starting to peek through the curtains. The room was cool and peaceful this early. She looked at Dee who laid in front of her, sleeping like a baby. She couldn't help feeling guilty for enjoying her time with him, especially when she knew her brother would still be looking for her. Dee had told her they only had one cell phone and one truck, but he didn't mention if any neighbors could help. She was going to ask him when he woke up.

Dee's eyes opened slowly a smile broke out across his face. "Good morning, sunshine."

"Good morning. Thank you for everything last night."

"It was nothing. I'm glad I could help."

"I was thinking. I really enjoy being here with you. There's just something about you that draws me to you. But I feel kind of guilty laying around with you while I'm sure my brother is out looking for me. I know you only have one truck and one phone, but what about any of your neighbors? Could any of them possibly help?"

"Our closest neighbor is about five miles away. That's a good hour and forty-minute walk. On your bad ankle, I didn't want to suggest it. Nor did I want to leave you here alone."

"Oh yeah, that makes sense. I guess I have to wait until your brother gets back and we put your plan into action."

"I guess that would be the best option. You've got at least another three days stuck with me," Dee pulled her close and kissed her.

This time, she didn't stop him.

THE WRONG PATH

Tommy sat at home in his room. His mom's chronic kidney disease was getting the best of her these days. She was too sick to get out of bed today so he took care of the cooking and cleaning. His mom couldn't eat much so he just cooked for himself. Being so worried about his mom and his girlfriend, he didn't eat much either. He hated the position he was in and wasn't sure what to do. He was suddenly startled by his phone ringing. He fumbled his phone and quickly picked it off the floor.

"Hello?"

"This is Tommy, right?"

"Yes, who is this?"

"That doesn't matter. I called you the other day. If you help me, I will make sure your mom gets dialysis or a kidney transplant. You up for it?"

"And if I don't agree to help you?"

"Then your mother and girlfriend will die. The choice is yours."

"The choice?"

"Who lives and who dies; your mother or girlfriend?"

Tommy felt he was in an impossible situation. He didn't have any blood family other than his mom, but he also considers Clayton and Ri'Lynn family. Ri'lynn was strong and wouldn't go down without a fight, his mom didn't have much, if any, fight left in her. Besides

Clayton would find Ri'Lynn before whomever this was, was able to actually kill her.

"Okay, fine. I'll do it. What do I need to do?"

"Smart boy. The hard part is already done. I just need you to make sure to lead Clayton in the wrong direction. Tell him she's probably in another town or whatever. I don't really care. I just need to make sure my son doesn't go around the lake him and I used to fish at."

So he was talking to Adam. "Okay, but how will I know you'll actually help my mom?"

"When are you going on another search with Clayton?"

"In two days. He's out now I'm sure, but I needed to be home with my mom because she's getting worse."

"You will know that I'll stick to my word, before your next search."

The line went dead. Adam's last words send a chill to his spine. Tommy knew he was a bad guy and felt horrible for agreeing to help him. He knew Adam would probably kill Ri'Lynn if he got the chance. Tommy was one hundred percent sure his friendship with Clayton would be over; his sister meant everything to him. Not only would his friendship end, so would his relationship with Ri'Lynn and he couldn't blame either one of them.

Maybe he should call Adam back and tell him he won't do it. If he did that, his mom would die. He would be completely alone but Clayton and Ri'Lynn would help him get through it, wouldn't they? He didn't have much of a life because all of his time was spent taking care of his mom. He wished he had someone to talk to about this because he didn't know how to get himself out of this mess without losing the people who mean the most to him. Tommy suddenly felt sick and ran to the bathroom just in time to vomit up the small breakfast he just ate. Was it bad milk or because he was worried sick? He wasn't sure.

****

"Come on, you move like a grandpa," moaned Clayton as he waited impatiently for Tommy in the car. "I want to be in the woods by sun up."

"I'm coming, I'm coming. I still think we should go to the woods on the other side of town by the lake."

"Why? My dad always goes to the one I'm talking about."

"That's my point. If he's behind this, he knows you are going to be helping look for Ri'Lynn. So he's not going to have her in a place you will know. He'll go somewhere different. Maybe even to a different town."

"You're right, man. Sorry, I'm not thinking clearly. I'd be so lost without you, Tommy."

Tommy just smiled. He felt horrible betraying his best friend the way he was, but he had no choice. If he didn't do this, his mom would die and he couldn't live with that. He knew both Clayton and Ri'Lynn would probably hate him after this whole thing was over, but everyone would be alive.

Clayton drove in the opposite direction like his friend suggested. He wanted to be in the woods by sun rise. He wanted to spend all day looking for his sister because he didn't know how long the police would keep looking for her. The detective on the case told his family they would keep looking but they weren't able to keep sending out search parties. It was up to them to find Ri'Lynn and bring her home. Clayton knew she was probably scared, especially if she was with Adam.

Clayton texted Derek to let him know he changed locations as they pulled up to the parking lot of the walking trail. He was so thankful for both Derek and Tommy for helping with the search. He wouldn't stop looking until his sister was found; dead or alive. He prayed with all his might that it would be the latter.

Back at the house, Derek sat with his legs hanging off the side of the bed. He thought about how Clayton had been out looking for a couple hours already. It really bothered him that he wasn't out there helping. Ri'Lynn hadn't been in his life long, but she was his daughter and he was supposed to protect her. Today was their family day; a day they do something together as a family. They've been doing family nights for over a year and all really enjoyed it.

However, Derek didn't know how much he would enjoy swimming at the public pool when his daughter was missing. He rubbed his eyes before quietly getting dressed and making his way into the kitchen to get started on breakfast. He jumped a little when he saw his family sitting around the table, dressed.

"Morning guys. Y'all scared me," he admitted, rubbing his head.

"Sorry honey, but we knew how bad you wanted to go searching with Clayton so we decided we would surprise you and would go, too."

"But today is our family day."

"Exactly. We will spend our day helping look for Ri'Lynn, as a family."

Tears started to run down Derek's cheeks. He couldn't believe how amazing his family has been through all of the craziness since Ri'Lynn came into their lives. He couldn't help but feel slightly guilty for putting them through it, too.

****

When Ri'Lynn woke up, Dee was already awake playing with Little Foot.

"Good morning," she said as she sat up in his bed.

"Good morning. Hope you don't mind my company. My brother had to go pick up the guy he's working for. We won't be able to get you home today."

"If he went to pick him up, they are gonna find out I'm gone!" Ri'Lynn jumped up and started pacing.

"Calm down, it's gonna be okay," Dee tried to reassure her.

"Please don't tell me to calm down because if he's working for my stepdad, it will not be okay. Can I just use your phone to call my brother? He can just come and get me."

"I uh...my brother and I share a phone, remember?"

"Ugh. That's right. Why do two grown men need to share a phone?"

"We don't have a lot of money," Dee admitted, as he walked to the window and looked out.

Ri'Lynn felt bad so she walked over to him and put her hand on his arm. "I'm sorry, that was rude of me. I didn't mean to be a jerk."

"It's okay, Ri'Lynn. I know you are scared of your stepdad. I don't know how, but I will do whatever I can to make sure you get back home to your brother."

"But, doesn't that mean betraying your own?"

"Maybe and I'm okay with that. He's been doing these stupid jobs for big pay outs instead of keeping a real job. He's gonna end up in jail or worse. I have to try to save him even if he doesn't want to save himself."

"You and your brother are complete opposites. You are nothing like him. After this is all over, I'll talk with my dad. Maybe him or my stepmom could get you a job in town."

"You'd do that for me, after my brother was the one to kidnap you?"

"If I make it out of this alive, I will owe you."

Ri'Lynn kissed him on the cheek; Dee blushed. He turned and faced her and pulled her close. "Is it wrong of me to say that I wish you didn't have to leave?"

"Is it wrong I feel the same way."

"You do?"

"It's been a couple of weeks since I first knocked on your door. I thought I would be dead by now, honestly. Either by the hands of my stepdad or starvation. Being here with you makes me feel safe. I don't know if it's because I was completely alone and isolated for a good month before, or what."

"I hope you don't regret what we've done," admitted Dee, hanging his head.

She grabbed his face between her hands, "I don't regret a minute of it. If I messed up my relationship, that's on me. I did it. At the same time, I'm not the same Ri'Lynn I was before I got taken. Who knows if Tommy and I even mesh together anymore."

Without saying another word, Dee kissed her and held her body against his.

Ri'Lynn pulled away, "I want to take a shower before we go there,"

"Oh... um, yeah of course."

"Dee, don't worry. I want you just as much as you want me. I just want to shower first."

He smiled and watched her head off to the bathroom.

Ri'Lynn could feel her heart racing. She had never felt so much emotion being around a person. Tommy never gave her butterflies like this. They had made out a few times, but that was nothing compared to her and Dee making out. Tommy and her hadn't had sex yet either. She turned on the water and slid in, deep in thought.

She stood in the hot water to let it massage the yellow greenish bruises that stamped her body. Dee filled her mind. She wondered what he would be like as a boyfriend, a real boyfriend. One that didn't live in the middle of nowhere and wasn't keeping her hidden in his closet. Ri'Lynn giggled at the thought, then suddenly the shower curtain was pushed open. Ri'Lynn quickly turned to see Dee standing there, butt naked, dick hard as a rock.

Ri'Lynn knew this was a bad idea but she couldn't stop herself. She grabbed his arm and pulled him into the shower with her. As the water rolled down his chocolate, muscular arms she could feel herself wishing for him. Before she could act on her feelings, he grabbed her and started kissing her as his hand massaged her breasts. He pushed her against the shower wall and held her there as he kissed all over her body.

Ri'Lynn loved every kiss, every touch. She enjoyed every moment of them together and silently begged for it never to end. But every time, it did end. With the hormonal beast tamed, guilt took its place trying to make her regret what just happened. Although, Ri'Lynn didn't regret what happened between them, she did feel bad for cheating on Tommy.

She began to think about Tommy. Did he still consider them dating? Was he waiting for her? Was he helping look for her? All these questions made her start thinking about exactly how long she'd been missing. Was it two months? Longer? Were the police still looking for her?

Her mind raced and made the room spin. One thing she knew for sure: Clayton wouldn't give up until she was home. Ri'Lynn had to do whatever it took to get home, even if that meant walking the five miles to the neighbor's.

A LITTLE CLUE

The whole town came out to help look in the woods for Ri'Lynn to give Derek's family a chance to rest. Clayton and Tommy headed back to the house while Derek and the others went to grab food. Tommy sat his phone on the couch and headed to the bathroom. Clayton's phone was dead and he needed to call Derek, so he went to grab Tommy's. He saw a message that sent chills down his spine.

"Clay, you good bro? You look like you've seen a ghost."

Clayton looked down at the phone in his hand, then back up at Tommy. "What is going on?"

"Huh? What do you mean?"

"What have you done, Tommy?" Clayton yelled.

"Whoa bro, you need to calm down. I don't know what you're talking about."

"My phone was dead. I was gonna use yours to call Derek. Then I saw this message," Clayton threw the phone to Tommy.

Good job with the wrong directions, kid.

"Clayton…" started Tommy.

"Stop, just stop. If you had something to do with my sisters disappearance,I swear."

"You think I had something to do with it because of that message?" Tommy yelled.

"Yes, I do. You led me astray. I wanted to go to the area my dad and I knew well, but you talked me into going on the other side of town. Sounds like you lead me in the wrong direction on purpose."

"Seriously Clayton, do you realize how crazy this sounds?"

"It does sound crazy, that's why I can't believe you'd do anything to endanger my sister!"

"Clay, Ri'Lynn is my girlfriend! I had nothing to do with her disappearance."

"Then what was that message about?" Clayton yelled.

Tommy didn't say anything right away. He just looked at Clayton. "I can't tell you. Not right now."

"Get out. Get the hell out of this house!"

Tommy didn't object, just took off out the front door and ran past Derek and others. Everyone was happy and laughing but it all came to a halt when they saw the end of Clayton and Tommy's fight.

"Want to tell me what just happened, son?" Derek asked softly.

"I honestly don't know. I saw a message on Tommy's phone and snapped."

"What message?"

"It said *'good job with the wrong directions, kid.'* It wouldn't even have bothered me if Tommy hadn't been so adamant about looking in the woods we looked in instead of by the lake like I wanted to."

"So you think Tommy lead you away from the lake because he knew your sister was there?"

"I don't know, maybe. I just didn't think anything of it until that message. It's been almost six months since she's been gone. If he knows anything and is keeping it from me, I might do something stupid. No, I lied. I *will* do something stupid."

****

Ri'Lynn lay on Dee's chest, his arm around her. She listened to his short breaths and his heartbeat; for a few minutes she forgot about everything. All of a sudden, Dee jumped out of bed.

"My brother's home."

She quickly grabbed Little Foot and they hid in the closet. Her heart was pounding, scared at what was about to happen next. She jumped as the bedroom door was flung open and it hit the closet door.

"Dee, she's…it smells like sex in here. Did you have a girl over?" questioned Ty.

"Yeah, she left though."

Ty gave him a pat on the back and was walking out of the room when something caught his eye. He walked over to Dee's dresser and bent down, picking up Ri'Lynn's dirty clothes.

"Where did you get these?" whispered Ty frantically.

"I dunno."

"Dee, have you been down to the shed?"

"No, I haven't been down there. Why? And why are you whispering?"

"Dee, don't lie to me!"

"I'm not lying. Ty, what's going on?"

"I went to the shed and the girl is gone. Dee, that guy is gonna kill me when he finds out. I've got to find her."

Dee didn't say anything. His heart was racing. He didn't want to give Ri'Lynn up, but he didn't want his brother to be killed. Before he could figure anything out, Ri'Lynn stepped out of the closet.

"Dee, what the fuck?" Ty looked at Ri'Lynn, shocked.

"I can explain…"

"Boy shut yo mouth. Let me think for a second."

Dee grabbed Ri'lynn's hand and squeezed it tight.

"How long has she been in your closet?"

"About two weeks."

"Fuck," he turned to Ri'Lynn, "How did you get here?"

"I just walked and walked until I saw your house. I knocked on the door and Dee let me in."

"Shit. Okay. We gotta get you out of here. Once I get you out of here safely, I want to explain myself."

Ty left the room, Dee and Ri'Lynn followed with Little Foot in her arms. They heard a truck pull up out front so Ty rushed them to the back door. Before Ty could even step foot on the porch, a man Dee had never seen before stepped into the room.

"Who the hell are you?" demanded Dee.

"Dee, don't," Ty warned.

The man tilted his head slightly to the left, squinted his eyes and said, "I'm about to be your worst nightmare."

He grabbed Dee by the back of the neck and pulled him out into the living room. Ri'Lynn had ran back to the closet unnoticed. Tears formed in her eyes and her body shook. Adam was here. He was out of jail and was at the same house she was at. Would Dee give her away? Would Ty?

Ri'Lynn tried to think about what she should do, she peeked out of her hiding spot and looked at the window. Maybe she could get it open and make a run for it. Quietly, she crept out of the closet and walked to the window. She lifted it slowly and was about to climb through when she heard Dee scream. She paused, tried to listen to what was happening.

"He said he didn't know who you were talking about. Stop it before you hurt him," yelled Ty.

"I don't give a damn about hurting your brother. You were supposed to do a job. I told you there would be consequences if you couldn't do it."

"Then take it out on me, let him go!"

"Now, what fun would that be?" smirked Adam.

He took out a knife from his pocket and pressed it against Dee's arm. "Where is she?" he asked again.

"I don't know."

Adam pressed the knife into Dee's arm causing him to let out a scream, a small amount of blood seeping through the skin. "If you don't tell me where she's at, it won't stop."

Dee didn't say anything and Adam didn't stop. Scream after scream, Ri'Lynn listened until she couldn't take it anymore. She took a deep breath and walked out of the bedroom, into the kitchen. Ty was the one to see her first, his eyes big and mouth dropped open. When Dee saw her, he shook his head no and nodded towards his room, signaling her to go back. She didn't.

"Adam, stop," she demanded.

"Holy shit. Look who it is," he said laughing as he turned around.

"Ri'Lynn go. Get out of here," Dee yelled.

She ignored him and directed her full attention to Adam. "What do you want, Adam?"

"To make you pay for what you did, of course."

"Let Dee go and we can talk about it."

Adam stood there and didn't speak or move. He took one step towards Ri'Lynn and she immediately tensed up. Adam then quickly moved behind Dee and put a knife to his neck.

"No, don't," both Ty and Ri'Lynn said.

"Why do you care so much for this guy, Ri'Lynn?"

"Because he has helped me."

"But his brother is the one that kidnapped you."

"Yes, but you are the one who paid him. This is your fault. When I get home to Clayton, he will be pissed."

"You're right, he will. But not pissed at me. Pissed at Tommy."

"Why would he be pissed at Tommy?"

"Because he helped me with your kidnapping," taunted Adam.

"He did...he did what?"

"I found out his mom was sick and needed a kidney transplant but there was no donors. I told him if he helped me, I'd make sure his mom got that kidney."

"Ho...how did he help you?"

Adam stepped from behind Dee and dropped the knife. He smiled, enjoying this all too much. "He left you alone after school so Ty here could grab you. Now he's making sure Clayton stays on the opposite side of town, far away from here. Knowing my son, he's going to try coming around the lake we always used to go fishing and would eventually find the shed I put you in. So poor little Tommy had to make a choice: help you, or save his mommy. You see who he chose."

Ri'Lynn stood in front of the man who was determined to break her. Tears ran down her face and those tears weren't just for her. She couldn't imagine what Tommy was going through. She wasn't mad at him for wanting to save his mom. She was mad at him for wanting to save his mom at her expense. She was upset he didn't come to her. He could have told her, he could have warned her or something. Ri'Lynn was upset because she didn't want his mom to die, but she didn't want to die either!

"Let Dee go and we can go wherever you want," Ri'Lynn said.

"I don't think I want to do that," replied Adam.

Adam turned quickly and slammed the knife into Dee's leg. Dee let out a horrific yell. Ri'Lynn rushed to his side as Little Foot rushed from the hallway and attacked Adam, drawing blood of his own. Adam kicked him off and was going to stab the dog when Ty stepped in and knocked him down. This further enraged Adam. Ri'Lynn noticed this and quickly untied Dee and helped him to his feet.

"Run," screamed Ty. "I'll hold him off."

Putting half his weight on Ri'Lynn, Dee limped out of the kitchen as fast as he could; Ri'Lynn pulled him along. Little Foot ran right in front of them and jumped into the truck. Once at the truck, Dee yelled to his brother to come on. Ty gave Adam one last punch and was halfway to the truck before they heard it; the loudest sound either of them had ever heard.

Ty stopped moving. His eyes looked down at the same time his hand went to his stomach. He pulled his hand back and it was covered in blood. Looking back to his brother, he mouthed "I'm sorry" before he dropped to his knees in slow motion and took his last breath.

"NO!" Dee screamed from the truck as he tried to get out.

"Dee, you can't. It's too dangerous. You can't. We have to get out of here."

Adam started firing shots at the truck.

"Go Ri'Lynn, GO!"

Ri'Lynn put the truck in drive and floored it. Adam had ran out of the house firing the remaining shots from his clip into the truck. Little Foot jumped down into the floorboard and Dee sat there almost lifeless. Ri'Lynn began to shake and cry as she sped away leaving one crazy mad man and one man clinging onto his last breath behind them.

REUNITED AT LAST

Clayton was laying in his bed watching Netflix, unable to sleep. It was late, and like every night, everyone else in the house had gone to bed hours ago. His phone started to vibrate, startling him. The number that blinked across his screen wasn't familiar to him but ever since Ri'Lynn had been missing he answered all calls.

"Hello."

"Clay."

"Ri...Ri'Lynn? Is that really you?"

"Yes, it is. I need you to meet me at the hospital."

"Hospital? Are you okay?"

"Yes, I'm fine. Just meet me there please. I'll tell you everything."

"Okay, I'll be there," Clayton leapt from his bed and quickly put his shoes on.

"And Clay?"

"Yeah sis?"

"Please, don't bring Tommy."

She hung up. Clayton ran into Derek's room.

"Derek, wake up! Ri'Lynn called, she's safe and wants us to meet her at the hospital."

"Is she okay?" asked Angela.

"She said she was."

Turning to Derek, Angela placed her hand on his cheek. "Baby, you two go and get her. I'll stay here with the boys."

"Are you sure you don't want to come?"

"Yes, I don't want to wake them especially since we don't know what kind of condition she's in."

"Okay honey," Derek kissed her and left.

"Derek?" Angela called.

"Yes?"

"Bring our girl home."

At the hospital, Ri'Lynn never left Dee's side as they examined his wounds. She made sure he was taken care of before letting them look at her ankle. When she was patched up, she headed right back to Dee's room. He had lost a lot of blood and would need to stay overnight.

"How are you feeling?" she asked.

"I'm...I'm okay."

"Dee, I'm so sorry about your brother. I wish we could have saved him, too," tears fell from her eyes.

"It wasn't your fault, Ri'Lynn." he squeezed her hand.

"It kind of was. If it weren't for me leaving, your brother wouldn't have gotten..."

Dee placed his hand on her face, wiping the tears that fell from her eyes. "Please don't blame yourself. My brother choose his own path. Most of the time he was a total asshole, but he was my brother and he meant well. He was my only family. My parents couldn't get him on the straight and narrow path and no matter how hard I tried, neither could I. If it wouldn't have been this situation, another would have got him caught up, too."

"I still wish I could have helped save him, too. Thank you for keeping your promise and helping me get home."

"I told you I was going to help get you home and I stick to my word."

"I'm sorry for getting you in this mess, too."

"Nah, my brother brought this mess home for us. Besides, I could handle it. I wouldn't have been able to handle it though, if you would have been the one getting hurt."

Dee pulled Ri'Lynn down to him and kissed her. That kiss held more passion than before. Ri'Lynn could feel it held pain and fear too.

"I know you have a boyfriend to get back to Ri'Lynn, but I can't help that I have strong feelings for you."

"Actually, I don't have a boyfriend to get back to."

"Do you believe what Adam said?"

"I honestly don't know what to believe. His mom is sick. He never knew his dad so he and his mom are really close; he would do anything for her."

"Including giving you to the man that raped you?"

"That's the part I don't understand. Why didn't he just come to us? We could have helped him. We could have figured something else out. I just… I don't know. But I have to go meet with my brother. I will be back."

"I'll be right here."

Ri'Lynn kissed him on the cheek and headed for the door. "And Ri'Lynn?"

"Yeah?"

"I'll wait for you."

Ri'Lynn smiled and walked out of his room knowing how much truth that statement held. She walked down the hallway heart beating faster with each step. She turned the corner and saw her dad and brother sitting there in the lobby waiting for her. When Ri'Lynn's eyes locked with Clayton's, tears fell and she took off running to him, she almost made him fall as she jumped into his arms.

Clayton looked her over as he asked "Ri, what happened?"

All eyes were on her as she told them everything. From what happened at the school, to the shed, to Little Foot who was waiting in the car, to Dee. She told them how Adam killed his brother and how he used Tommy's sick mom to convince him to help.

"Wait, Tommy did help him?" asked Clayton.

"Adam said he told Tommy to lead you away from your fishing spot and his mom would get the kidney transplant she needed. He basically wanted Tommy to choose who lives or dies."

"I can't fucking belive that," Clayton spat.

"Mouth boy," warned Derek. "Ri'Lynn, if you aren't hurt, why are you at the hospital?"

"I want y'all to come meet Dee. Adam stabbed him in the leg and he lost a lot of blood. He's the only reason I'm back here now. Adam would have killed me if it weren't for Dee and his brother."

They followed Ri'Lynn into Dee's room. Once they were all in, she introduced everyone. They all talked for awhile before Derek walked up to Dee and extended his hand.

"I am so sorry to hear about your brother. We would like to pay for his funeral."

"That isn't necessary, Sir."

"Dee, you brought my daughter back to us. You bet your ass it's necessary."

"Okay, I appreciate that, Sir. Thank you."

Ri'Lynn told her dad and brother she wanted to stay the night here with Dee. With Clayton agreeing to stay too, Derek allowed it. After he left, Ri'Lynn told Dee to get some rest while her and Clayton went to the lobby to talk. Clayton just had to know every detail that she didn't share with her dad.

"Okay, now tell me everything," he said once they were settled. "Starting from the beginning."

"First, tell me how long I've been gone."

"It's been six months, closer to seven."

"Holy shit. Okay well that day I got taken, some little girl came up to me saying she was lost and trying to get to the library. Someone else came up behind me and put something over my face to knock me out. I woke up a couple times while we were in the van moving, but I couldn't keep my eyes open long enough to see anything."

"When I woke fully, I was in some abandoned shed with a big ass chain around my ankle. I also found Little Foot in this shed and he never left my side. We escaped the shed and walked for what seemed like hours. We slept in a Weeping Willow and I hate crickets; lots and lots of crickets. Finally, we found a house and Dee opened the door."

"I went inside and he patched my ankle and fed us. I quickly found out his brother was doing a job for some guy and he's the one who took me. He hid us in this little place inside his closet. We had a plan to take his brother's car and he was going to bring me to you, but his brother left for a few days and we couldn't. When his brother returned, he was with Adam who was pissed I wasn't in the shed."

"When Ty, Dee's brother, figured out I had been there, he was going to help get me out of there. Adam grabbed Dee and started to torture him. I was about to jump out of the window and make a run for it, but I couldn't just leave him after all he'd done. Anyway, I went and tried to plead with Adam to let him go. Of course, that wasn't an option for him. I think prison did something to your dad, Clay. He wasn't the same person. He was more...I don't know. His eyes were cold and he scared me more than he did before."

"Ty started fighting him so me and Dee ran. As Ty was coming to join us in the truck, Adam shot him. Then he emptied the rest of his clip into their truck, but I floored it and got us the hell out of there."

"Damn. Ri', I don't even know what to say. What did he say about Tommy's help?"

"Oh yeah. He told me that he had asked Tommy to make sure I was alone after school that day and to make sure he led you in the wrong direction of the lake you guys would fish at."

"I knew it! I wanted to go check around that lake, but he talked me out of it. Then I saw a weird message on his phone and sorta went off on him about it. He said he couldn't tell me what the message was about, so I kicked him out."

"Apparently, Adam told him he had a donor lined up for his mom if he would help. But what I don't understand is why he didn't come to us, or at least you. We could have helped him!"

"We sure as hell would. I'm gonna kick his ass for giving you to Adam, gift wrapped."

"Don't kick his ass, Clay. He was faced with an impossible decision. I'm not mad at him for wanting to save his mom. I'm mad at him for doing it at my expense."

"That's my point!"

"Well, if it makes it any better, I kind of cheated on him with Dee."

Clayton was quiet for a minute then he nodded his head and smiled. "I could feel something was there. I'm not judging you. You've been gone for what seems like forever and he was helping you stay alive and eat. Then you find out your boyfriend sold you out. I'd be pissed if you stayed with him honestly."

Ri'Lynn shook her head and pushed her brother on the arm. "I missed you so much."

"Ri, I never stopped looking for you."

"I know."

****

The funeral Derek had for Dee's brother was beautiful. Since they didn't have any family, Derek had people from his job and the police department come. He knew Ty was the one to actually kidnap his daughter, but he died trying to save her; he was forgiven. He wanted to do it for Dee because he was the real hero here. Without him, he might not ever have seen his daughter again.

"Baby, I think Dee really appreciated the funeral. I am so proud of you for doing that for him." Angela said as she rubbed her husband's arm affectionately.

"It was the least I could do. I wish I could do more. His brother was all he had now the poor kid has nobody."

"What if we can do more?"

"What are you thinking, my love?"

"He can't go back to that house. Why don't we help him get an apartment here in town? He could work at Remington Square as a leasing agent with me. I mean, if he wanted."

Derek kissed his wife. "Baby, you are amazing! We should go talk to him about it."

Angela smiled and followed her loving husband into the living room where they were watching TV. "Hey Dee, have you thought about what you are going to do next?" she asked.

"Uh. I haven't really. I guess go back to the house and clean it up and try to sell it."

"How would you feel about living in town?"

"I would love to. We just had one vehicle so I just always worked around the house."

"I am a manager at this apartment complex in town. I could get you a job and an apartment, if you'd like."

"You guys really don't have to do that. You have been kind enough to me already."

"Dee, we want to. If it wasn't for you and your brother, Ri'Lynn might not have come home to us. You can take time to think it over if you'd like. The offer will stay there as long as you need it to."

"Thank you so much."

They all sat in the living room and watched a movie like one big, happy family. After the movie was over, all of them went their own ways. Clayton and Dee went with Ri'Lynn to her room and continued hanging out. They all sat on her bed listening to music and talking when all of a sudden the door swung open and in stepped Tommy.

"Wow. I cannot believe you're actually home," Tommy rushed over and hugged RiLynn.

He noticed how close her and Dee were sitting and quickly tightened. He spat, "I would ask why you didn't call me, but I see you're busy."

Tommy turned his nose up at Dee, and stormed out getting all the way to his car before Ri'Lynn could get him to stop. Clayton and Dee ran after her, but stopped on the porch to give them their space.

"Tommy, wait up for a second," called Ri'Lynn. "I'm sorry. You're right, I should have called you to let you know I was okay. I just wasn't ready yet," she admitted, forcing him a small smile.

"Ready yet? What did you have to get ready for? I'm your boyfriend!" Tommy threw up his hands in the air.

"I know but..."

"But what, Ri? You were too busy shacking up with that guy?" he interrupted. "Were you even kidnapped or was this just some ploy to break up with me?"

Shocked and appalled, Ri'lynn's mouth dropped wide open. "Okay first off, I know you're upset I didn't call you, but you know if I wanted to break up with you, I would have just talked to you."

"Do I know that, Ri? I don't even know you anymore," Tommy shrugged his shoulders.

"You're right. You don't know me because a lot has happened since you last saw me. I understand you are hurt and for that, I am sorry." Ri'Lynn paused making sure Tommy was looking right in her face then said, "You also know I was really kidnapped because Adam said he had you help him."

"I uh...I'm sorry," Tommy paused as Clayton walked up. Looking down at the ground, Tommy admitted, "He said he could help my mom. I didn't know what else to do."

"You could have came to us bro. We would have helped you," interjected Clayton.

"How Clayton? How could y'all have possibly helped?" Tommy asked, his body tense.

"I don't know honestly, but it wouldn't have been giving my sister to my dad gift wrapped with a bow."

"There would have been nothing you could have done! I tried and tried to figure out a way out of it but I couldn't find one."

"We would have figured it out. We could have helped your mom got the help she needed. I'm sure Derek and Angela could have helped, too," Clayton said.

"If I would have said something, y'all would have messed it up and my mom wouldn't have had the surgery," yelled Tommy.

Clayton placed a hand on Tommy's shoulder. "How did that work out though, Tommy? You helped my dad kidnap my sister and you still lost your mom."

Tommy saw red. He punched Clayton in the face, causing him to stumble back before Tommy went in for another swing.

Clayton blocked the punch and grabbed him by the collar of his shirt. "I would have done anything I could have to help your mom *and* make sure my sister was safe. I wouldn't have done anything to jeopardize my sister." Clayton let go of Tommy's shirt. "I'm not gonna hit you back. I understand both of our emotions are high. I can't exactly understand why you did what you did because I don't like it and I really wished you'd came to me for help. But I get it, you were trying to save your mom. I need some time to cool off, but I think we can keep our friendship."

Tommy stood there not too sure what to say. Clayton told him he'd text him later and headed back inside. Dee sat on the porch watching Tommy closely as Ri'Lynn finished talking to him. He didn't trust Tommy could remain calm and wanted to be there if anything happened.

"Like my brother, I understand you did it to save your mom. I was your girlfriend. I am your friend. I don't understand how you could just make it so easy for Adam after all he had done to me. You know for a fact, we would have figured out a way to help both your mom and me," Ri'Lynn said as tears ran down her face.

"I can't make you understand, Ri."

"Why didn't you just lead my brother to me if you knew where I was? You could have made Adam think you helped him, but you helped us both."

"I didn't know exactly where he was keeping you. I was just told to keep Clayton away from the lake him and Adam fish at."

"I was walking to the car when someone knocked me out and grabbed me. When I woke up, I was chained to a pole in some shed; ankle killing me. I was alone. I was scared. When I slept, all I did was have nightmares about never seeing my brother or you again. I also had nightmares about you all moving on and forgetting me. Getting back to the two of you is what kept me going, kept me pushing to get out of those woods no matter how hurt my ankle was. Now, finding out you had a choice -- not between saving your mom or me, but between keeping this secret or getting some help, and you choose to keep it really fucks me up."

"Where does that leave us?"

"To be completely honest with you Tommy, I no longer trust you. I can't date a guy I don't trust. Like my brother, if you give me time we can be friends, but nothing more."

"Are you really breaking up with me because of me choosing my mom over you? Or is it because of him?" Tommy asked, voice cracking pointing at Dee..

"Dee has nothing to do with my decision to end our relationship. And it's not about choosing your mother over me. It's about you letting Adam, the man I fear, the man who hurt me more than anyone, get to me."

"He didn't hurt you, though Ri. He just had you held in the woods."

"He didn't just have me held in the woods, Tommy." Ri'Lynn showed him her black and blue ankle that was finally healing. She lifted her shirt, showing all the cuts, scrapes, and bruises that had lived on her stomach for these seven months. "He might not have physically hurt me this time, but I was alone in the woods. Scared, with no food, no water, no shelter. I was always looking over my shoulder worried he would find me and kill me. And he *was* going to kill me."

"Man, I'm sorry. I didn't realize all of that happened. But why is he here though?" he asked, pointing at Dee.

"Not sure why it matters, but Dee is here because not only did he help bring me home, his brother died saving my life and his home is a crime scene."

"Couldn't he stay somewhere else?"

"There isn't anywhere else."

"Why not a hotel or something?"

"I don't know why it matters, Tommy."

"It matters because I don't want him sleeping in the same house as you," yelled Tommy, fists balled up.

"That isn't up to you," Ri'Lynn said, softly.

"Are you sleeping with him?"

Ri'Lynn didn't answer his question. She just looked at him, hoping he wouldn't press the issue. There was no need to hurt him more than he already was. With losing his mom and all of this, she knew he wasn't keeping it together well. Out of nowhere, he began screaming and yelling at her, causing her to drop to the ground, knees bent to her chest. Ri'Lynn rocked back and forth as Tommy called her all kinds of names and was telling her how much he hated her. Dee ran to Ri'Lynn, making her stand, and as he turned to take her inside, Tommy grabbed his arm, stopping him.

"Let go of my arm, please," Dee said, his voice even toned.

"Let go of my girlfriend," spat Tommy.

"You are upsetting her. She needs to go inside and you should leave."

"Who do you think you are?"

"I'm her friend," said Dee, pulling his arm from Tommy's grasp.

With Tommy done yelling at her, Ri'Lynn turned to say something to him when his fist landed on her face, making her fall to the ground. Dee spun around and punched Tommy square in the jaw.

"I...I didn't mean to. Ri… I am so...sorry. I was going to punch Dee and you got in the way."

"It's fine, Tommy. Now please, go home."

Tommy did as Ri'Lynn asked and she and Dee went inside. Clayton was livid when he saw her face with a little blood on it, but after Ri'Lynn begged him to let it go, he agreed. She cleaned the blood from her face and went to her room, not mad at Tommy. She knew he was hurting and didn't mean to hit her. She told Dee and Clayton who were hanging out in the living room that she was off to bed, climbed into bed and within minutes, passed out.

Once Clayton went off to bed, Dee made himself comfortable on the couch. Ri'Lynn's stepmom said she would get the spare bedroom cleaned so he could sleep in there until he figured out what he wanted to do. He already knew he would take Angela up on the offer to work at the apartment complex. His decision wasn't made because he wanted Ri'Lynn to be his. He wanted her to be a part of his life. And the rest of her family as well.

During the middle of the night, there was a loud scream. Everyone woke up and ran out of their rooms trying to figure out where it came from. Dee knew it came from Ri'Lynn's room and was in her room in seconds, grabbing her up like he'd done so many times before.

"What's going on?" asked Derek, busting into her room.

"It's a nightmare. She has them pretty bad."

Angela went to tuck the boys back into bed and let them know she was okay, but Derek and Clayton stayed put. Ri'Lynn's screaming had stopped, but she was still talking in her sleep and shaking.

"How long will this last?" Clayton questioned.

"It depends on how bad the nightmare was honestly. Some lasted a long time with lots of screaming and fighting and others only a few short minutes."

"What do you do to help her? How do we make it stop?" asked Derek, worry written all over his face.

"I just hold her so she doesn't hurt herself. I try to wake her up by giving her a slight shake. When she does wake up, she will be panicked because the nightmare felt real, so I reassure her it was just a dream. Then we would talk about it and she would go back to sleep."

"Wow," Derek said scratching his head. "You've really taken care of her. I appreciate it more than you know."

"Don't mention it. You guys can head back to bed, I'll stay up with her until it passes."

They thanked him and headed back to bed. Dee kept trying to wake her and finally her eyes opened, but this time she wasn't panicked; she was calm. Smiling at him, she sat up.

"Another nightmare, huh?"

"Yeah, only this time you woke everyone in the house."

"Oh my gosh. That is embarrassing."

"Don't be embarrassed, you've been through a lot. I told your dad I'd sit with you until it passed."

"Can you stay in here with me?"

"Only if I sleep on the floor."

"No way! I want you to hold me like you did before."

"Okay, but no funny business in your dad's house."

GETTING ON WITH LIFE

Life was finally getting back to whatever normal was going to be for them now. Both Ri'Lynn and Clayton finished school online. Dee had started working at the apartment complex and had his own place. Although Clayton and Tommy were working on building their friendship back, Ri'Lynn just wasn't ready yet. Tommy accepted it and Ri'Lynn was thankful.

Ri'Lynn and Clayton were just hanging out at the house one afternoon. She noticed for the last few days he had been acting a little different lately, but she couldn't put her finger on why. She decided now would be the perfect time to ask and just went for it.

"Clayton, are you okay?"

"Yeah, I'm good. Why do you ask?"

"You just seem a little off lately, that's all."

"Oh uh, I just have a lot on my mind."

"What's going on? Talk to me."

"While you were away, I found out something. It slipped my mind and I forgot all about it until a couple weeks ago. Ever since then, I've been trying to figure out how to tell you."

"Tell me what, Clay? You don't have to be afraid. After everything I've been through, I can handle it."

"There's no way to prepare you for what I'm about to say, so I'm just gonna say it."

"Then spit it out already," Ri'Lynn laughed.

"Mom is alive."

"Wait. What?" she asked, her mouth dropped to the floor.

"Mom faked her own death. She's been living with nuns."

Ri'Lynn started laughing. She laughed so hard she cried. She couldn't catch her breath which made Clayton laugh too.

"Why… are we ...laughing?" he asked between giggles.

"Because I wasn't expecting that. The last thing I thought I'd ever hear was mom being alive… living with nuns. How did you find out?"

"You're taking it much better than I did. She just showed up here at the house and told Derek and I. I was really pissed off at her. And to be honest, I still kind of am."

"I understand that. Are you mad that she lied? Or mad that she just showed up ten years later and dropped it on you?"

"Both. I just can't seem to understand why she lied. I don't get why she stayed hidden for ten years, why she didn't at least come for us. I know she was afraid of Adam, but I don't feel like that is a good enough reason to abandon her kids. She could have taken us with her."

"I feel like your dad would have raised hell if she, or anyone, took you."

"I mean, yeah, you're right. But I just… I don't know. Aren't you upset at all?"

Their conversation was interrupted by multiple bangs on the front door. They exchanged glances and Clayton got up to answer it. He was about to yell at whoever it was on the other side when he opened the door to see his best friend standing there, tears running down his face. Tommy didn't say anything. He hung his head and pointed to an ambulance leaving his house. Clayton didn't have to say anything either, he just grabbed his keys and the two boys rushed off to the hospital.

Ri'Lynn was left standing there worried about Tommy's mom. Their friendship wasn't restored yet, but she cared deeply for his mom. She hoped things were okay and headed off to her room thinking about her own mom. Was she mad at her for faking her own death? It was strange. If Adam was abusive to her as well, Ri'Lynn could understand why she did it; to escape. What bothered Ri'Lynn the most was that their mom kept her being alive a secret for ten years. Couldn't she have gotten a hold of them and let them know somehow?

What am I supposed to do now? How am I supposed to start a relationship with my mom who I thought was dead?

****

"What am I supposed to do now?" Tommy asked, running his hand through his hair.

"I… I honestly don't know, man," admitted Clayton. "Do you have any family that you could call?"

"No, I really don't. My mom had a falling out with her family when she got pregnant with me. I didn't grow up knowing any of my family."

"I can ask Derek and Angela. They will know what to do."

"Do you think he will be willing to help me after what I did?"

"He's angry, not a dick. I'm sure he will, he's a good dude."

"I really appreciate you coming here with me."

"Tommy, you are still my best friend. You made a stupid decision, but your heart was in the right place. You wanted to save your mom."

"Yeah, well look where that got me. My mom just died and I lost not only my relationship, but my friendship with Ri."

"If you give Ri'Lynn time, I know y'all friendship will go back to normal. I am really sorry about your mom, though. I can see if you can stay the night tonight and we can talk with Derek and Angela tomorrow if you want?"

"I think that's a good idea. I really don't want to be alone right now."

Clayton called Derek who of course said Tommy could stay. He helped Tommy pack a bag then they headed home and Clayton got him settled in his room on the cot. Tommy just curled up and lay down so Clayton left him and went to find his sister.

Ri'lynn sat in her room at her desk when her brother came in and plopped down on her bed. She laughed as his body bounced up and down on her bed, but she caught a glimpse of his face, seeing the tears she quickly stopped.

"Clayton, what's wrong?"

Her brother didn't answer.

"Clay, talk to me."

Clayton sat up and looked at his sister. "She didn't make it."

Ri'Lynn's stomach dropped. She felt sick. Her hands began to shake and tears rolled down her cheeks. She instantly began to worry about Tommy. What would happen to him? Where would he go? Was he going to be okay?

"Where's Tommy?"

"He's in my room asleep."

"What's he going to do? Does he have any family he can stay with?"

"He said he doesn't. He doesn't know what to do. I brought him back here so we can talk to your dad and Angela and see if they would have any ideas on how to help him."

"I'm sure they will."

"Tommy was afraid they wouldn't help him because of what he did."

"I'm sure they will. Actually, I'm gonna go talk to my dad right now."

Ri'Lynn took off out of her room and found her dad working in his office. She knocked on his door before she went in.

"What's up, Ri?" asked her dad.

"Are you busy? I'd like to talk to you about something."

"No, I'm not. What's on your mind?"

"Tommy's mom just passed away. He's alone and has nobody; no other family or anything. I was wondering if you'd help him with what he needs to do next?"

"That's too bad about his mom. How do you feel about him? Are you upset with him still? Or have you forgiven him?"

"He was my best friend, aside from Clayton, before we started dating. I really do care about him. I'm not mad at him, I never really was mad, mad. I was just hurt, honestly. I loved his mom and I want to be there for him and help him get through this."

"You are such an amazing person, sweetheart. Of course I will help with whatever I can. Where is he now?"

"He's in Clayton's room asleep."

"Good, I'm glad he agreed to sleep here tonight. We can talk tomorrow about what he's going to do next."

Ri'Lynn ran over and gave her dad a big hug. "Thanks so much, Dad."

"You're welcome, sweetheart."

"One more thing, Dad. What do you think about my mom being alive?"

"Oh Clayton finally told you about that, huh?"

"Yeah, he did. I just honestly don't know what I should do."

"I think the first thing you should figure out is how you feel about it. Are you angry? Hurt? Once you figure out what you're feeling, then decide if you want her in your life. You were pretty young when she 'died', so she's practically a stranger to you. You don't have to rush into making a decision. Anything you or Clayton decide, I will fully support."

"I don't know how to sort through my emotions around this just yet. I plan on taking my time with figuring it out, though. My focus is helping Tommy right now. Thanks Dad."

She rushed out of his office before he could say anything back. She quickly made her way to Clayton's room to check on Tommy but he wasn't in there. Confused, Ri'Lynn headed toward her bedroom when she heard crying coming from the den. It was dark except from a small sea of light from the moon that came through the curtains nobody closed all the way. Sitting there on the couch was Tommy. His knees were to his chest and his arms wrapped tightly around them. He looked so small sitting there like that. Ri'Lynn's heart ached for him.

"Tommy," she started.

"Oh, um. Hey Ri," he said, wiping his eyes.

"Mind if I join you?"

"Not at all," he said and patted the couch next to him.

"Tommy, I am so sorry. I am heartbroken. I can't even begin to imagine what you're going through. I just want you to know that you're not alone. Clayton and I will be here for you and help you in anyway we can."

"I appreciate that. Thank you."

"I mean it," she said, placing a hand on his leg. "I know things have been kind of rocky for us, but I am always here if you need me. I loved your mom; she was the sweetest."

"She was pretty amazing. She always loved you and was so happy when we started dating. I don't know what I'm going to do without her. I miss her so much, Ri."

"I know you do. I miss her, too. We will figure it out. I asked my dad if he can help you figure out what to do next."

"You... you did?"

"Of course I did. He said he'd help. Now, it's been a crazy day. Why don't you go try to get some sleep?"

"Yeah, I should probably try. Thanks for everything."

Ri'Lynn hugged him tightly then walked to her room quickly. It was after midnight by the time Ri'Lynn actually got in bed. She lay there unable to go to sleep. Her mind kept wandering back to the last time she saw Tommy's mom. She remembered cooking dinner while she sat at the table and they talked. Ri'Lynn could feel the tears coming so she rolled over and tried to think about something else, anything else.

****

Dee had agreed to let Derek and Angela help him with the job and apartment and he was glad he did. He couldn't imagine what it would be like if he would still be in that big old house alone. Alone, he would be totally alone. Here, he wasn't alone at all and that was a different feeling. A feeling that felt strange to him until he met Ri'Lynn. He didn't understand how meeting a person for the first time could bring him so much heartache and joy at the same time.

Ri'Lynn and her family have been so amazing and helpful. Dee hadn't ever been in love before, but he felt like he could fall for Ri'Lynn. As he tried to get his mind off of her, he decided to keep unpacking some of his things. His apartment was still bare, but he hoped to make it more homey soon. Before he could unpack another box, there was a knock at the door. He glanced at his watch, slightly nervous as to who would be stopping by after one o'clock in the morning.

After glancing through the peephole, he quickly unlocked the door and opened it. "Ri'Lynn, are you okay?"

"I hope I didn't wake you," she said, forcing a smile.

"Not at all. Please, come in."

Ri'Lynn followed Dee inside, glancing around his apartment. It was a cute little studio that was perfect for him. He still had unpacking and decorating to do, but she was glad he decided to move into town and let her family help him. It was the least they could do.

"Not fully unpacked yet, huh?"

Scratching his head, he laughed. "Nah, not really. I still need to go back out to my house and finish packing it all up, I just haven't yet. What's wrong? What brings you by so late?"

She took a deep breath, she blurts out, "I found out my mom is alive and today Tommy's mom passed away."

"Wait. You mean to tell me your mom, who you thought was dead for most of your life is alive? How is that possible? How did you find out?"

"I guess when I was missing, she showed up at the house and told Clayton she faked her own death to get away from Adam. She was living with nuns and just showed up to tell us everything."

"Wow. I can't believe that. How did Clayton take it?"

"He's pretty pissed off. He doesn't understand why she couldn't have told us, or took us with her."

"How do you feel about it?"

"That's what I'm struggling with. I don't know how to feel, exactly. Part of me wants to be mad at her. But I have also been on the receiving end of Adam's fists. I know how it felt to want to disappear, to leave and never come back. I know how she felt and I can't blame her for wanting to get away from him. I just wish she would have told us. We could have kept a secret from him. I would have done anything to see my mom one last time."

The tears rolled down Ri'Lynn's face. She couldn't stop them from coming. She cried for her mom, she cried for herself. She cried because she was angry, sad, hurt, and scared. She cried into Dee's chest, one of the safest places she's ever felt. He held her, running his hands through her hair like he did so many times before. It was as if he washed all her pain right out of her body.

She pulled herself together and changed the subject onto something else.

"Clayton and I can come help you pack up some more this weekend if you'd like. Maybe even bring Tommy if that would be okay?"

Dee's body stiffened at the sound of his name. "Are you… are you two back together?"

"No, we aren't. He just lost his mom. I feel like in a way, you guys are in a similar..."

"We are not the same," Dee snapped, cutting her off.

"Dee, I wasn't saying you were. I was saying you guys were in a similar situation. Both of you lost everyone and now have nobody."

"I have you," Dee said, pulling her close.

"And as much as you are going to hate this, so does he."

Dee walked away, tears forming in his eyes. He didn't like what he was feeling. Was it anger? No, it was much more envious than that. It was jealousy. He was jealous of Tommy being in Ri'Lynn's life. He wasn't sure why he was feeling this way, but he really didn't like it one bit. The feelings he had for her were no secret. What would he do if she chose Tommy over him? There would be no way he could stay here, no way this new life would stick.

"Dee, did you hear me?"

"Huh? No, I'm sorry. I didn't hear you. What did you say?"

"I said he is my friend and nothing more. I will always care about him as a friend, but there is no chance of him and I being anything more. Not only because of him agreeing to help Adam, but because my feelings I have for you are real."

Dee looked at Ri'Lynn and smiled. Before he could say anything back, she leaned in and kissed him. As they sat there on his couch, kissing with the moonlight coming through the window, he knew that everything was going to be okay, that everything was going to work out for him, for Ri'Lynn, for everyone.

ABOUT THE AUTHOR

Jessica was born and raised in the small town of Coffeyville, Kansas. Her lifelong passion for writing is what made her never stop fighting to reach her dream of becoming a published author. Author of Try Me Not and The Secret Teller, Jessica currently resides in Kansas City, Missouri with her boyfriend and seven-year-old stepson.

Keep up with current works by following her on
Facebook: @GrundyWriter
Twitter: @GrundyWriter
Instagram: @GrundyWriter
Blog: avoidingthebackspace.wordpress.com

Jessica Grundy

Made in the USA
Middletown, DE
07 April 2022

63739944R00083